D1111379

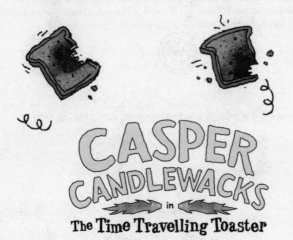

CASPER CANDLEWACKS

in

The Time Travelling Toaster

First published in Great Britain by HarperCollins *Children's Books* 2013
HarperCollins *Children's Books* is a division of HarperCollins*Publishers* Ltd,
77-85 Fulham Palace Road, Hammersmith, London W6 8JB

Visit us on the web at
www.harpercollins.co.uk

1

CASPER CANDLEWACKS IN THE TIME TRAVELLING TOASTER
Text copyright © Ivan Brett 2013
Illustrations © Hannah Shaw 2013

Ivan Brett asserts the moral right to be identified
as the author of this work.

ISBN 978-0-00-741161-0

Printed and bound in England by
Clays Ltd, St Ives plc

MIX
Paper from
responsible sources
FSC C007454

FSC™ is a non-profit international organisation established to promote
the responsible management of the world's forests. Products carrying the
FSC label are independently certified to assure consumers that they come
from forests that are managed to meet the social, economic and
ecological needs of present and future generations,
and other controlled sources.

Find out more about HarperCollins and the environment at
www.harpercollins.co.uk/green

CASPER
CANDLEWACKS

in

The Time Travelling Toaster

IVAN BRETT

Illustrated by Hannah Shaw

HarperCollins *Children's Books*

More adventures with

Casper Candlewacks in Death by Pigeon!

Casper Candlewacks in the Claws of Crime!

Casper Candlewacks in the Attack of the Brainiacs!

For Amy

Chapter 18

The End

PS Oh dear. This book seems to have developed the capability of time travel. It's actually a pretty common thing, especially when there's time travelling going on within the book's pages. The story gets ideas of its own, you see, and soon you've got Chapter 1 following Chapter 12, Chapter 4 hiding in the middle of Chapter 5, and Chapter 7 fighting barbarians somewhere in the

Middle Ages. It's a nightmare, I tell you.

Listen, the best thing to do is just ride it out. I'll fill you in as we go along, OK?

Chapter 2

The Bus Stops Here

Oh, that's close enough. I mean, ideally you'd start with Chapter 1, but not much happened, really. There was this big dog that wouldn't stop eating muffins, but it's not central to the story. So let's just begin from here.

"Ladies and gentlemen, this may be the proudest moment of my life."

Mayor Rattsbulge wiped a greasy tear from his enormous cheek and licked his finger.

"To be standing in the shadow of such a majestic structure, and to have that structure *named after little old me*? Well, few people in this world could feel as proud as I do now. To have our very own bus shelter here in Corne-on-the-Kobb." The mayor trembled. "To enjoy its many uses, such as, well, actually… what does a bus shelter *do*?"

A murmur of confusion spread through the crowd. Beards were scratched, shoulders were shrugged. The 107-year-old Betty Woons gasped and almost rocked her wheelchair over, but then her smile wrinkled up and she shook her head. This was a problem. Nobody had a clue what a bus shelter did, and if nobody knew, what was the point in having one?

In truth, this sort of thing happened quite a lot around these parts. You see, Corne-on-the-Kobb was what's known in the trade as A Village of Idiots. With an average IQ of just under fifty-six, and an average reading age of minus three, the villagers of Corne-on-the-Kobb weren't the shiniest spoons in the drawer. If left to their own devices they'd often end up stuck in a tree, buried neck-deep in a vegetable patch or sleeping inside your washing machine. But that's exactly what makes Corne-on-the-Kobb brilliant.

"Somebody must know," groaned Mayor Rattsbulge. "Where's that clever lad? The one with the face. Oh, what's his name – Camper Catalogue or something. He'll know."

The name spread through the crowd like Chinese whispers.

"Find Catcher Capricorn!"

"Where's Candy Calculator?"

"Get Calcium Carbonate!"

At the very back of the crowd, Casper Candlewacks sighed. "You mean me?"

Heads nodded eagerly and the crowd parted to let Casper through.

"Ah, just the fellow," said Mayor Rattsbulge, ruffling Casper's scruffy blond hair. "Got any idea what this chap actually does?" He gestured to the shiny new bus shelter.

The wide-eyed crowd looked on expectantly. Noise trickled down to silence as they waited for the boy's verdict. Even the pigeons stopped pecking to listen in.

Casper pointed inside to the wooden seats. "Erm... you sit here to wait for a bus."

"HOORAY!" The crowd exploded with joy and Casper was promptly forgotten.

Not being an idiot in a village full of idiots was a full-time job, as Casper would tell you (between bouts of averting disasters and saving days). It meant late nights, early starts and a terrible pension package. But deep down, Casper loved it.

He wandered off to sit on a bollard just as the mayor asked, "What's a bus?"

Casper picked up a soggy copy of Corne-on-the-Kobb's weekly newspaper, the *Daily Kobb*, which floated on a puddle. On the front page Casper could still read the headline, the story that everyone had been talking about (until Mayor Rattsbulge announced the opening of his bus shelter):

THE *Daily Kobb*
BANKRUPT BLIGHTS TO SELL BLIGHT MANOR

Below the headline was a picture of Blight Manor, a once-great mansion, now old and crumbling, with missing windows, half a roof, and walls that had buckled and bent more than a bent buckle.

The Blight dynasty existed long before Corne-on-the-Kobb had even been thought of. A baron of Blight ruled the Kobb Valley after the Norman Conquest, and the family have held the seat with their cold-knuckled fists ever since. But in the years that passed, the Blights' hold on the Kobb Valley slipped, their lands shrank and their finances dwindled. The last Lord Blight died under mysterious circumstances – after his daughter poisoned him. It's not that mysterious, really. Now Lady Lobelia Blight and her daughter, Anemonie Blight, resided in Blight Manor, desperately clutching at the embers of their once-great empire. With the sale of Blight Manor, the lordship would slip away and the estate disappear, leaving nothing in its place but a nesting-place for the pigeons.

A steel-capped black leather boot slammed down on the soggy paper, splashing a muddy puddle all over Casper's trousers.

"Oy!" Casper jumped back to avoid more wetting. Then he looked up to see the owner of the boot... and shivered. "Anemonie Blight. What d'you want?"

"It's all lies, Candlewacks!" shrieked Anemonie, her oh-so-noble pointy nose red with shame. "How many times do I have to punch you before you understand that?"

Casper shuffled back further as Anemonie advanced, fists clenched. "Look, I don't care how much money you have."

"Lots of money!" she shouted. She had long dark hair and a threatening squint. "Rooms full of it, in fact. An' if you say we don't, I'll bite you."

"OK!" Casper held up his hands. "I believe you! You're still rich."

Anemonie stopped and smirked, but her eyes stayed steely cold. "Good. Make sure you tell everyone." As she turned to leave, she spotted a two-pence piece on the ground and bent down to snatch it like a pigeon to a breadcrumb. She straightened up and looked around to check nobody had seen.

Casper pretended to watch a tree.

Once Anemonie had stomped round the corner, Casper gave a sigh. However much he despised the little bully and her pointy nose, watching

Anemonie's downfall was a pitiful sight. A few generations back, a Blight's packed lunch would contain caviar sandwiches and cartons of alcohol-free champagne. But now Anemonie was eating free school lunches and getting caught stealing cabbages from Mrs Trimble's shop.

The crowd from the ceremony was filtering away gradually, although many villagers had formed a long line stretching from the bus shelter and away down the road. As old Betty Woons trundled by, she gave Casper a knowing wink. She always did. It was unnerving.

"Casper! Casper!" A sooty-haired, lumpy chap in a blue boiler suit and sponge shoes came galumphing out of a garage at the end of the street. He spotted Casper, gasped, and galumphed in his direction. He only fell over twice on the way, which was a new record. "Casper, I did it! I really did it!"

"What did you do, Lamp?"

Lamp Flannigan, Casper's best and only friend, was red-faced and puffing from his run. He was eleven, the same age as Casper, with a dongle of a nose, wide, round eyes and a funny way of standing that always made him look as if he was about to sit down. He also had toes that glowed in the dark ever since he let a small family of fireflies live in his shoes, and the world's first elephant-repellent boiler suit. Lamp was an inventor by trade… but we'll get to that.

"I did my Time Toaster! Look…"

Lamp crossed his eyes and stuck out his tongue

with concentration as he fumbled around in the pocket of his boiler suit. Finally his eyes lit up and he pulled out a blackened, crumbling piece of toast.

Casper waited for the toast to do something amazing.

It didn't.

"So…" Casper shrugged. "It's just toast."

"Not just toast, Casper," Lamp grinned, relishing the words on the tip of his tongue. "This is toast from *the future*."

Chapter 3

The Time Toaster

Casper was a good fifteen centimetres taller than Lamp – and a good fifteen centimetres better at spelling, for what it's worth. Casper was a dab hand at sums, a keen reader and he could list the kings and queens from 1066 to the present. Lamp could just about list the numbers from one to two, but he struggled to open books the right way up and he didn't even know when history was.

Casper's clothes were scruffy hand-me-downs from his dad's rock-band phase, while Lamp only wore his boiler suit. When it got dirty, he wore it backwards to save on washing. The two made an unlikely pair, but because they'd saved the village three times since June, and it was only a quarter past eleven on the sixth of October, nobody was complaining.

Lamp's one and only strong point was inventing, but, boy, was he good at it. He'd invented just-add-water moustaches, hind wheels for donkeys and a torch that glowed dark in the day. The thing is, when Lamp Flannigan says a piece of toast is from the future, you'd do well to believe him. He's not normally wrong about that sort of thing.

Lamp's house sat at number 1 Corne Approach, a charming two-bedroom property, just a stone's throw from the new bus stop, complete with a garage, good access to the town centre and stunning views into the window of the house across the road.

But who'd want to look outside when the interior held such wonders? Lamp's garage was dark, gloomy and absolutely wicked. Here, amongst piles of scrap metal and buckets of leftover doorknobs, Lamp let his inventions take form. Today, at centre stage on the workbench, sat a brushed-steel, four-slot toaster with a dozen metal springs boinging outwards at jaunty angles, each with a watch face glued to the end. Most of the watches were cracked, bent or missing vital numbers, like three etc. The hands weren't turning, either, so Casper guessed they were just for decoration. Multicoloured wires sprouted from inside the toaster and wound about in scruffy coils, meeting again as they stuffed inside a digital alarm clock strapped on to the toaster's front face. A series of buttons ripped from Lamp's mum's cardigans had been installed in a long line below, each labelled with things like SEKUND, MINIT, and MUMF. "It's my Time Toaster." Lamp proudly patted it, making the little watch faces

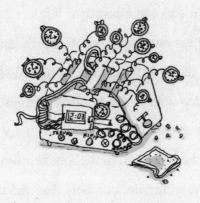

wobble. "It steals a piece of toast from any toaster through time and space."

"Oh…" Casper let that flow over him. "But why would you want toast from anywhere through time and space?"

"If you're hungry, of course."

"Couldn't you just make some real toast?"

Lamp blinked. "Didn't think of that. But listen, this is way better." He pulled out the crumbling slice he'd shown Casper earlier. "Sniff this."

He did. It smelt of toast.

"See?" grinned Lamp. He took a bite. "Mm, futurey."

Casper waited patiently while Lamp invented a jam magnet.

When the toast was finished and the jam wiped off the walls, Lamp licked his lips and said, "So. Fancy a slice?"

"I... er…"

"Me too!" Lamp bounced across the garage to his Time Toaster and twizzled some buttons.

"Ready?"

Casper took a few steps back and shoved on a motorcycle helmet that was lying on its side. "As ready as I'll ever be."

"Then *Let's TIME!*" Lamp did a heroic pose involving pointing one finger at the ceiling.

"Wait!" shouted Casper. "Can we think of a better catchphrase first?" He was worried that *Let's Time* would stick.

"Erm…" Lamp chewed on his tongue. "How about '*Let's Hope We Don't Get Sucked into the Time Vortex and End Up Getting Trampled On by a TRICERATOPS!!*'"

Casper shuddered. That was a hope that he too shared, but he didn't want to think about it every time Lamp made toast. "Shall we stick to the first one, then?"

Lamp nodded. "In that case, Casper, there's no time to lose. *Let's TIME!*" He pushed the toaster's lever down with a geeky flourish and the alarm clock went off. A dim, pulsing buzz came from the toaster's bowels. The watches began to tick round now, slowly at first, but speeding up and up, until the springs shook and the hands were a blur of minutes and hours.

Smoke poured from the machine, and Casper smelt toast. A lick of flame danced from the top of the slot, then a crackle and hundreds of little clangs as the whole machine shuddered and the watches clashed into each other.

The cloud of smoke engulfed Lamp and his Time Toaster. Casper coughed into his shirt, his eyes stung, the smoke plumed across the garage and surrounded him too.

"Lamp!" he coughed. "Has it gone wrong?"

Through the smoke Casper saw somebody stumbling about inventing a fire extinguisher, but there was no response.

"Turn it off!" Casper shouted. "Turn–" but his lungs filled with smoke and he bent double, coughing. He longed for fresh air, for a cool breeze, for a friend who didn't burn things down all the time.

Then… *SPRUNGG!*

Something popped up. The cacophony ceased, the flames died and the smoke began to thin. Through Casper's watery eyes he could see Lamp plucking something from the toaster's tray and blowing it out with sharp puffs. Little cinders still burnt at the corners, so he threw it to the floor and gave it a good stamp.

"You can have that slice," said Casper, straightening up and rubbing the ash from his eyes. "Not a big fan of stamped toast."

Lamp picked it up and gasped. "But, Casper, this isn't toast!"

"More like charcoal."

"No, no, look. This is writing! It says…" He scratched his nose, leaving a black smudge. "Casper, can I read?"

"Not often, no. Give it here."

The oily boy was right. He held out a charred strip of paper, yellow and curled and peppered with cinder holes. Most of the blackened bottom half melted away into ash as Casper took it, but some words at the top were still visible through the soot. A title, an author and a date.

Casper's brain twisted the wrong way up. "What? But…" He read the paper again. And again. He rubbed his eyes. He looked at the date, and the name, and the title. Then he pinched himself. He asked Lamp to pinch him. He asked Lamp to punch him. He asked Lamp to stop punching him now, because six times was quite enough.

"What's it say, then?"

Whichever way Casper read the paper, the words written on it were impossible. Firstly, it seemed to be an article written… *written*… by Lamp. This in itself was beyond belief. Only once in his life had Lamp spelt a word correctly. (He wrote 'fish',

34

which is more of an achievement when you don't know that it took him a week and he was trying to spell the word 'the'.)

But more importantly, the date said *18 November 2112*. That would make Lamp 111 years old when he wrote it. Now, Betty Woons was 107 and going strong, but she didn't get blown up nearly as often as Lamp. And anyway, Betty was probably lying about her age. She'd been 107 for as long as Casper had known her. Sure, she was old, but in all likelihood she'd lost count at around 80 and just picked her favourite number.

And even if Lamp *had* grown to 111 years old and learnt to write, why would he discredit his own time machine, of all things? It was Lamp's ultimate goal! With this toaster he was halfway there! Why ever would he criticise something like that?

"I think your machine's broken, Lamp."

"Can't be. If it was broken then this light would come on." He pointed to a green bottle cap on the top of the alarm clock marked BROKKIN.

"But this is written by you, in the future, and it says the Time Toaster should never have been invented."

"Don't be silly," chuckled Lamp. "I can't write."

"Well, that's what I thought."

"So what's that writing mean, then?"

"I haven't a clue." Casper chewed his lip, but that didn't help at all.

Lamp thought for a minute, then snorted. "We should go and find out!"

"To the future?" Casper's heart beat faster. "But how?"

"All we've got to do is climb into the Time

Toaster. Then the me in the future will pull the switch." Lamp was already trying to force his foot into the tray. "Gimme a push, Casper."

"Lamp, you'll never fit!" Casper gave his friend a shove, but his toes barely passed the lip of the toaster. "You're just not toast-shaped."

"I could be," Lamp piped up. "As long as I bring some glue with me, I could travel in slices."

"Not sure that's wise."

"But I want to go time travelling, Casper! I could be a knight, and a spaceman, and – ooh! – I could be a postman!"

"You could be a postman now."

"Not a proper postman, Casper. In the olden days they rode horses and fired guns at deserts."

"That's a cowboy."

A gasp came from the garage doorway.

Both boys spun round and one squeaked. There stood Anemonie Blight, her greedy eyes wide. She pointed a black-nailed finger at the Time Toaster. "Wassat, then?"

"Nothing," snapped Casper. "Go away."

"Not until you tell me what it does," the girl smirked. "Fly, does it? Will it do yer homework?"

"It's not finished," lied Casper, "and even if it was, it still wouldn't do anything."

"Actually –" Lamp stepped forward proudly, clasping his hands together and closing his eyes like a museum curator describing Picasso's bogey – "it's a time machine."

Anemonie's ears pricked up.

Casper's heart leapt.

Lamp's tummy rumbled, so he took a bite of toast.

"Time machine, is it?" Anemonie's body had tensed, her eyebrows raised.

"No!" cried Casper. "You heard him wrong. He said… erm… prime gravel. That's it! It makes gravel for your garden path, that's all."

"No, it doesn't," Lamp frowned. "It makes time travel."

Casper winced. He jabbed his friend twice with an elbow, to the rhythm of *Shut up*, but by the look on Anemonie's face, he knew it was too late.

"The things I could do with a time machine," the girl murmured, inching forward with a wild look in her eyes. "Go back and buy last week's winning lottery tickets; take a telly back in time and pretend I invented it…" She giggled. "Or I could just sell the time machine. Reckon it's worth a hundred pounds at least."

"A hundred pounds?" chuckled Lamp, shaking his head. "Not likely. My Time Toaster's more valuable than all the money in all the piggy banks in all the world."

That was enough. Pound signs flashed in Anemonie's eyes and she launched at the boys, fingernails first.

Lamp spun protectively and grabbed the Time Toaster while Casper stepped forward to block Anemonie's path. She deftly dodged him, leaping to one side and bouncing at Lamp. Turning away just in time, Lamp found himself holding the Time Toaster at arm's length as Anemonie pushed into him, screaming with envy.

"Lamp! Over here!" Casper was unmarked at the entrance to the garage, and he'd played enough rugby to know this was a good thing. "Chuck it!"

Anemonie lunged, but not in time to deflect Lamp's mighty lob as the Time Toaster soared into the air…

…and landed with a *CRASH!* about fifty centimetres in front of Lamp's feet.

"You broke it." Anemonie sneered with disdain at the crumpled heap on the floor. "How'm I gonna sell a big lump of broken metal?" With a huff, she stomped from the garage, spitting on the floor as she left.

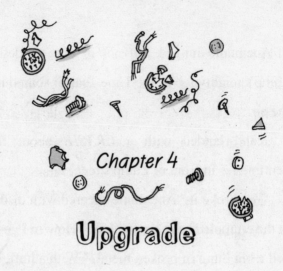

Chapter 4

Upgrade

Once Anemonie's steel-toed footsteps had faded far into the distance, Casper began to pick up the shattered pieces of what used to be Lamp's Time Toaster, and place them on the central workbench. "So… how bad is it?"

Lamp hadn't spoken yet. In fact, he hadn't even moved. He was still in the same stretched position as he had been when he threw the Time Toaster, like a statue of the world's worst ballerina. Slowly, he let his arms drop and his gaze fix on the pile of scrap. At the top of the pile, a single green light was flashing: the bottle cap marked BROKKIN.

Lamp smiled weakly. "At least that bit's still working."

And so the boys began the painstaking task of fitting the Time Toaster's pieces back together. Casper had to pop over to Mrs Trimble's shop to buy two more pots of glue and a yo-yo. By the time he came back, the queue at the bus stop had mostly filtered away. Sandy Landscape, the village gardener, who'd joined at the very back, was now taking his turn to sniff the brand-new seats and knock on the glass walls. Happy all was in order, he murmured some words of approval and strolled back up the street.

Casper smiled as the muddy man passed.

"Mornin', Casper." Sandy Landscape doffed his floppy hat. "You ent seen me goat, 'ave yer?"

"Have you checked your goat pen?"

Sandy looked impressed. "Now that I ain't. But I shall check there next. Thankee, Casper." And he trotted off to look in the place where he always found his goat.

Back in the garage, Casper found Lamp doing a little jig. "What's going on?"

"I did a clever!" Lamp wiggled his hips and waved a spanner around. "Remind me to thank Anenemy for breaking my Time Toaster."

"Why on earth would you want to thank her?"

"I think I put it back together wrong. Now it sends stuff rather than receives it."

"That's good!" said Casper. "I guess. Still

44

just toast, though…"

"Not if you don't want toast. I can send anything!"

"As long as it fits in the toaster."

"Not any more." Lamp waddled across to a dark corner of his garage and returned with a tartan tin full of old biscuits. He stretched two red wires from one of the many holes still left in the Time Toaster and stuck them to the tin with two squares of tape. With a flourish of his hand and a shout of "*Let's TIME!*", Lamp tugged down on the toaster handle and the machine coughed into action.

When the smoke cleared this time, however, there was no toast. In fact, rather than anything new, something was missing. The biscuit tin, and the biscuits inside it, had completely vanished.

At first Casper thought Lamp had scoffed a

secret snack under the smokescreen, but then he would have had to eat the tin too, and tins aren't that tasty.

"Someone in caveman times is gonna have a lovely treat," smiled Lamp.

The biscuit tin had gone. Through time. Casper found himself short of breath. "But this is... *amazing*! Will it send anything?"

"So far I've tried it with a colouring pencil, that biscuit tin and one of my shoes. I think that covers most things."

Casper hadn't noticed until then that one of Lamp's sponge shoes was missing.

"All you need is a big enough container to put stuff in, and it'll send that stuff through time! Including us!" Lamp couldn't help but start his jig again.

"Including us? But that means…" Casper's mind raced with the possibilities. "But this is huge!" he gasped. "Lamp, this is *proper time travel*, not just prehistoric toast."

"I know!" Lamp beamed. "I'm going to go and cuddle a Viking!"

"We've got to be careful here."

History was being made in this garage. Casper just wanted to make sure they knew exactly *what* history they were making before they blundered through time and killed Henry VIII or something. "Do you have any control over where we go?"

"Course!" said Lamp.

"And if something goes wrong we could come right back?"

"S'pose," Lamp shrugged.

"So all we need is a big enough container.

Something that can carry us both, and the Time Toaster itself, through time."

"Yep; it's got to be big and made of glass."

"Why glass?"

"So we can see where we're going."

Casper thought for a long second. "Then I know just what we can use."

Lamp lugged the Time Toaster under one arm. "Is it far?" he huffed.

"Just round the corner."

One step out of Lamp's garage and a turn to the left, and Casper could see it: Corne-on-the-Kobb's oven-fresh bus shelter.

Glinting in the autumn sunlight like Mrs Trimble's lost glasses, the brand-new bus shelter was the perfect vehicle for Lamp's Time Toaster. Casper trailed down the road after Lamp, picking up the bits that fell off his friend's invention.

"Do you really need this?" asked Casper, scooping up a party blower that had dropped out of a singed crack in the toaster's base.

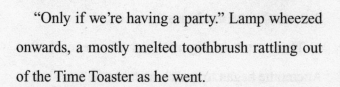

"Only if we're having a party." Lamp wheezed onwards, a mostly melted toothbrush rattling out of the Time Toaster as he went.

The installation was simple enough, but it took time. Lamp had to glue the Time Toaster snugly to one glass wall and feed the red wires into the timetable board. Just as he was about halfway through, the shape of a girl appeared round the corner.

"Oy!" came the ear-splitting screech of Anemonie Blight. "Wotcha doing?"

This time Casper was quick off the mark. "Don't tell her, Lamp! Pretend it's something else."

"Got it," grinned Lamp, turning to call back to Anemonie. "It's not a time machine any more, Lemony. It's a…" Lamp's tummy rumbled. "Casper," he whispered, "I can't think of any things that aren't time machines."

There was a long moment of silence before Anemonie began to march towards the bus shelter.

"Oh, cripes." Casper's heart raced as his eyes flicked from Lamp's unfinished upgrade job to the stomping girl. "If you can't get this working, we have to run now."

"I can do it," Lamp assured Casper. "Just takes time, that's all."

"We don't have time!" cried Casper. Anemonie had passed Lamp's garage now. She was close enough for Casper to see her necklace of wolves' teeth that clacked together as she stomped.

"How much time don't we have?" asked Lamp.

"Most of it!"

"Gimme that time machine!" roared Anemonie, her teeth bared hungrily. She was wrinkling her pointy nose, her fists clenched and shaking, her eyes filled with the fire of a thousand suns. "I want it! It's mine!"

"Hurry, hurry, hurry!" Casper hopped from foot to foot like a cat in a fireplace.

Lamp stood back proudly, wiping oil down the legs of his boiler suit. "There. Now all we need to do is choose a date." He sucked his finger thoughtfully, looking at all the buttons he could twiddle.

"Anything!" shouted Casper. "Just choose your favourite numbers and let's go!"

"I don't know many numbers."

Lamp licked his lips and turned the dials to *21/10/2112* (he wasn't a fan of anything past three) shoved down the handle and grinned. "Hey, Casper."

"What?" He couldn't keep still. She was metres away now. "What is it?"

"Let's TIME!"

The Time Toaster churned as it set to work, vibrating through the glass panes of the bus shelter until the whole structure began to hum. It was an odd noise, serene and formless, like a choir of ghosts who'd all forgotten the words.

Anemonie was close now. "Your bus ain't coming, Candlewacks," she smirked. "I'm gonna be rich!"

"It's working!" cried Lamp.

"Not quickly enough! Come on, come on…"

The air was growing cloudy, the glass singing more loudly, but Anemonie had reached the shelter and was barging towards the Time Toaster that was glued to the wall.

"Give it here. Hey, it's stuck!" Batting away Casper's protective arms, she tugged with all her might at the Time Toaster, planting one boot on the wall for purchase. "Nnnnngh!" she nnnnnghed, but it didn't break free.

The bus shelter screamed now, the air thick with the smoke from burning toast.

"It's doing it!" shouted Lamp over the din. "I told you it would, Casper!"

Casper's eyes stung. He coughed as the smoke filled his lungs and he backed into a corner.

"Whassit doing?" shrieked Anemonie. She carried on tugging at the Time Toaster, but her head was buried in her jumper to block out the smoke. "Is that you, Candlewacks? Who's burning?"

As the ground began to rumble, Casper lost his footing and fell on to a plastic seat. "Lamp! Is it broken?"

"We're travelling through the... which dimension is time again?" Lamp's voice was coming from the wrong side of Casper's head and he realised he was on the floor. "Whichever it is, it's a bumpy dimension," Lamp added.

"The smoke," choked Casper. "My eyes sting!"

"It's the mists of time!" Lamp took a deep breath. "Mmm, toasty."

Somewhere in the mists of time, Anemonie squealed. "We'd better not be time travelling,

Flannigan! If we end up in dinosaur times I'm gonna break your legs off and throw 'em to a T-Rex."

The bus shelter spun. Casper lost his sense of direction and bonked his head on the floor. Anemonie screamed, Lamp practised his handshake, Casper wished he'd had some lunch so he could throw it up, and then...

SPRUNGG!

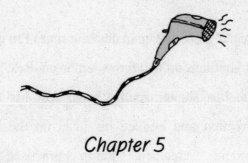

Chapter 5

Spot the Difference

The screaming was no more. The ground stopped shuddering and returned to its rightful place. Smoke still filled the air, but now it just hung there. All Casper could hear was his own coughing and the short, determined breaths of Anemonie Blight somewhere nearby.

"Well, I think that was a success," said Lamp, from somewhere.

Casper groped around on the floor until he found Lamp's remaining sponge shoe. He pulled himself up blindly, not quite trusting the ground beneath his feet. By the time he was standing, the smoke had thinned a little. He saw Lamp beside him, rubbing the soot from his face with an equally sooty hand.

"Did it… work?" Casper's eyes still stung and the smoke was thick.

"I thought the future would be less smoky," said Lamp. "Also, I hope they sell Time Toasters because mine broked."

Most of the watch faces had fallen off, there was a small fire licking out of one side and the alarm clock on the front had melted. Anemonie was still pulling at the Time Toaster, but the fight and the sense of direction had gone out of her. Dizzily, she tripped backwards, skittered around the smoky shelter, found an exit and fell through it.

"Future? This ain't the future…" murmured Anemonie. "Ooh, my head."

"What're you talking about?" Casper fumbled for the edge of the glass. His fingers found freedom and he staggered, coughing, out into… well… the very same place they had been before. There was Lamp's street in Corne-on-the-Kobb, the same wonky houses and cabbage patches, the same scruffy hedges and big glass bus shelter, smokier, but in the same place. Casper felt his shoulders droop. "She's right, Lamp. It didn't work."

Lamp bonked against the glass wall, bonked against the other glass wall, bonked against the first glass wall again, then emerged from the bus shelter in a cloud of smoke, rubbing his thrice-bonked nose.

"Oh."

If a face had ever looked disappointed, it was Lamp's face right then, all droopy-eyed and slack-lipped.

Casper scoured the scene, hoping to see a hover-car or cyber-donkey or something to prove the Time Toaster had worked, but there really was nothing out of the ordinary.

"Hang on," Lamp chirped, suddenly brighter. "There *is* a difference. My nose hurts more in the future!"

"Isn't that because of all the bashing it's taken?"

"Oh. You're too clever for your own good, Casper." Lamp scuffed his shoes at a pebble, but it didn't explode, or soar into the distance, it just skittered away like pebbles would do in the present day. What a disappointment.

"Tell you what." Casper clapped Lamp on the back. "We'll let the smoke clear, have a biscuit and try inventing something else."

Lamp smiled weakly. "I like biscuits. Ooh, and water slides. Do we have any water slides?"

"Might do. Let's have a look in your garage."

"Wait up!" Anemonie's screech disturbed the peace. "Please don't leave… I mean… c'm'ere or I'll thump ya."

Casper looked back at the girl stumbling behind with fear in her eyes. But… fear? *Anemonie?* That was something he'd never seen before. "What's wrong? Are you scared?"

"Ha! As if I'd be scared!" Anemonie laughed cuttingly, but her eyes darted around as if she was looking for somebody. "It's just… it's all quiet. I dunno."

She was right. Corne-on-the-Kobb was as quiet as a trombone stuffed with socks. The only things Casper could hear were the dim hiss of Lamp's Time Toaster and Anemonie's heavy breathing.

But then Corne-on-the-Kobb often was quiet on a Sunday afternoon. *Perhaps everyone's asleep, or at church*, thought Casper. *Or asleep at church.* (That did happen a lot when Reverend Septum was preaching. Even the old vicar himself had been known to have a cheeky snooze in the middle of his own sermons.) But no, there was something odd about the village this morning. Did the air taste different? Was the ground bouncier? Were the trees a little greener or the houses a little taller? "It's probably nothing."

"Yeah," agreed Anemonie, "so stop being such a wimp, Casper." But she looked no happier. She kept looking over her shoulder and she wouldn't stop fiddling with her gold signet ring.

Lamp tugged open the rusty door to his garage and breathed in a gulp of the familiar air inside. "Home sweet home!" he cheered. "Who's for— Oh. I think someone's got angry in my garage."

"What?" Casper dashed over to join him by the garage entrance. "Oh my. What a mess." Clutter and broken gadgets littered the floor around Lamp's upturned fridge, its door hanging open and a swarm of flies buzzing about inside. The workbenches round the walls had lost legs or given way in the middle, tipping their smashed contents on to the floor. Dust covered every surface, dank water dripped from a hole in the ceiling and the cheese piano and lobster tank, which had taken up most of the floor space last time Casper looked, were nowhere to be seen.

Lamp sniffed at the chaos with a bewildered nose. "It's a bit messy. I'd better invent a big hoover."

"Hah!" cackled Anemonie as she caught the others up. "Couldn't have wrecked it better myself. Just look at that destruction! I should learn some tips from this job." She poked her pointy shoes around in the rubble, scratching her chin and occasionally nodding.

But in Casper's mind something didn't add up. "But we just left here a minute ago," he said. "It was fine. How could somebody cause so much havoc in so little time?"

VRMMMMMSKREEECH!

Casper spun round in time to see a sleek black convertible scream round the corner, brake violently, spin a shrieking circle with its front wheels locked and slam side-on into a lamp-post. Casper jumped backwards and Anemonie leapt for cover behind a pile of used doorknobs.

From the smoking car, a door was thrown open and two figures strutted out, both in smart suits.

"Are you guys all right?" shouted Casper.

A wirily built young man with a pointy nose laughed back. "Cracking piece of parking, Chrys," he announced. "Lucky we've got a dozen more in the garage."

The other stranger snarled – a girl, younger than her partner; she had short dark hair and a similarly pointy nose. She drew a black hairdryer from a holster on her belt and aimed it at Casper. "Stay where you are," she grunted. "This thing's loaded."

"What with?" chuckled Casper. "Hot air?"

The girl cocked her head, confused. "Don't joke with me. You know what this does."

"Course I do. My mum's got one. She uses it after a shower." Casper felt a little bolder now. Two kids with a crashed car and a hairdryer weren't much of a threat, however you looked at them.

"She uses it after a shower? On herself?" The girl's frown got frownier. "How odd…"

"Chrys!" roared the taller stranger. "How many times? Rule one – never turn your back on the enemy. Rule two – never engage them in small talk!" He rounded on the girl, turning his back on Casper in order to discipline her further.

Casper tapped the lad on the shoulder. "Can I help you at all?"

He whipped round, enraged. "DO NOT TOUCH ME!" Reaching for his own belt, the lad snapped a matching hairdryer from its holster and pointed it at Casper's head. "Don't you know who I am?"

"Not… exactly…" By this time, Lamp and

Anemonie had emerged from the garage and were watching the situation keenly. "Are you from… around these parts?" asked Casper.

"Around these parts?" The lad chuckled softly to the girl called Chrys, lowering his aim with the hairdryer. "I AM THESE PARTS!" The hairdryer was up again, closer this time, the end almost touching Casper's nose, and the lad's face shook with rage. "State your name and business or FEEL MY WRATH!"

Something about the way the lad held his hairdryer, how smartly he was dressed, the fact that he'd just crashed a sports car into a lamp-post, hinted to Casper that it might be best to tell this madman what he needed to know.

"I'm Casper Candlewacks."

A dirty smirk appeared on the lad's face. "And I guess that makes the fat lump Lamp Flannigan, does it?" He tilted his hairdryer at Lamp.

Lamp checked the name label on his boiler suit

and nodded.

"You think this is funny?"
The lad swooshed his hairdryer to
the left and pulled hard on the trigger.
A *WHOOSH* of hot air sent a slew of
breadcrumbs blowing from the bell, zooming to
the left of Lamp and scattering on the grass behind
him. Casper only had a second to snigger at the
hopelessness of the lad's weapon before a tearing
screech from the sky froze the laugh in his throat.

Dark shadows stretched from the trees and
lifted into the air with ragged wings. One screech
became one hundred as the air grew thick with the
flapping of feathers. Casper lifted his eyes just in
time to see clouds of shrieking birds blocking out
the sun as they soared and circled, screaming, then
plummeted down towards the patch of grass to

snap at the breadcrumbs.

Lamp screamed, spun and jumped for the comfort of Anemonie's arms, but missed and flew headfirst past her into the garage. Anemonie paid no attention to Lamp, watching the birds with her hateful eyes as if weighing up an opportunity, while the two smartly clad strangers chuckled to each other.

"Not laughing now, are we, *Candlewacks*?" laughed the lad, putting too much emphasis on the word 'Candlewacks' and doing bunny ears with his fingers. "You see, the local wildlife's got a little hungry recently. Fewer people around to feed them bread. And then we came along with these little things." He rattled the hairdryer to show there was plenty of bread left inside. "Just imagine, a smattering of bread over that little round face of yours." He smirked. "Dinnertime! And those beaks are ever so sharp, you know. So… you want to tell me your real name now?"

"What?" Casper's mouth was full of feathers and his mind was full of claws and beaks. (Not literally, of course. That would be bird-brained.) "I… er…" But he'd forgotten his name. All he could think about were the vulture-like abominations fighting for bread on the lawn. With savage beaks and dark wiry talons, the birds clawed for the breadcrumbs, pecking, scratching, cooing… *Cooing?*

Casper gasped. "Those are just pigeons?" The bread was long gone, as was the grass, but the birds still clawed away at the mud as if they'd not had a square meal, or a circular meal, or triangular, or any shape of meal at all, in years. Either that or they were digging for Australia. "But they're so…

savage," said Casper, disgusted. "And look at the state of their feathers. What's happened to them?"

The lad laughed bitterly. "Times are tough for all of us, not least the pigeons. When they sniff bread they get a little... frantic."

"What do you mean 'times are tough'? Times have never been better. Why, trade's booming at my dad's restaurant, Mrs Trimble has started stocking milk again and the mayor just opened our first bus shelter! Look, I don't know who you are, but—"

The hairdryer was pointing at Casper's head again, and this time he knew to shut up.

"What mayor? Which restaurant?" The lad's lip quivered. "You'd better stop lying, sir, cos my trigger finger's getting awfully itchy. So tell me again... who are you?'"

"I'm Casper!" Casper cried. "How can I make that any clearer?"

The lad looked like he was finding it tough not to explode. But then the girl called Chrys gasped, leant over and whispered something into the lad's ear. His face changed, softened, and he cocked his head to one side, blinking. His eyes flicked to Anemonie, and then to Lamp in the garage, and then back to Casper.

"I'm gonna ask you this only once, and your answer will directly affect whether you get eaten by pigeons or not. So tell me, *Casper*, what year is this?"

"Ooh! Ooh!" squeaked Lamp, who'd stuck up his hand and was now hopping on the spot. "I know this! Pick me!"

Was this a trick? Casper examined the strangers'

faces: snarling, doubtful, but deadly serious. Either they didn't know, which wasn't that unusual for Corne-on-the-Kobb, or it was a test. And with their hairdryers raised and loaded, the pigeons perched on nearby gutters watching the exchange hungrily, it wasn't one Casper wanted to fail. "Twenty twelve?" he said hesitantly.

The strangers shared a look, then turned back to Casper. "So it's true…" gasped the one called Chrys, staring at him as if he was encrusted with diamonds.

And just like that, the hairdryers were down and the lad had proffered a gloved hand for shaking. "Sorry about all that, old boy. Can't be too careful these days. I'm Briar."

They shook. Briar's grip was cold and glovey.

"Briar Blight."

Chapter 6

Family Reunion

Crunch. Briar Blight squeezed Casper's hand far too hard, pulverising his bones into soup. The lad smirked, but didn't loosen his grip. "And this is my sister, Chrysanthemum Blight, but she likes to be called Chrys. Pretty name, ugly sister."

Chrysanthemum smirked sarcastically at Briar.

Confusion and shattered bone surged through Casper's veins. "Blight?" He winced, pulled his hand free and turned round to see Anemonie stepping forward, grinning like a minx. "D'you know them?"

Anemonie ignored Casper's question and shoved straight past. "Blights, eh? Well, I've not heard of you, and I'm a Blight. I'm THE Blight. Anemonie Epiphany Hookworme Blight. Heir to Blight Manor, owner of a hundred slaves and the last hope for the upper classes. What're you, then? Second cousins on my dad's side?" She crossed her arms challengingly.

Briar's eyes grew wide. Next to him, Chrys watched Anemonie in awe, her snarly mouth agape. "Granny?"

Anemonie tipped her head back and guffawed. "HAH! What are you, stupid or somethink? You ain't my granny. I met both my grannies. None of

'em had *that* hedgehog barnet, and both of 'em are dead."

Chrys touched her hair protectively.

"What she meant to say –" said Briar, digging the steel cap of his boot into Chrys's ankle, which made the girl squeak – "is that your granny is our granny's first cousin's nephew's… er… dog. We're distant relatives, but just as posh, and we're well rich. Look."

Briar produced a black wallet with a gold rim from his suit pocket. He popped it open, pulled out a fat wad of banknotes between thumb and forefinger and cast them off into the breeze without a second thought.

The pigeons that had bank accounts swooped down to catch some cash in midair, but most of the notes fluttered away on the wind, up past the

trees and away.

Briar upturned his wallet and let a shower of coins clinkle to the ground. He stamped on the coins, threw his empty wallet over his shoulder, where it bounced off a hopeful pigeon and landed in a puddle. "What's it matter? I've got billions of quid in millions of wallets. I'd have thrown it away at the end of the day anyway. A Blight never reuses his wallet."

Judging by the sparkle in Anemonie's eyes and the glint in her nose, the girl was impressed. "Only a true Blight'd do something *that* wasteful. Welcome to the family."

"Yeah, thanks." Briar wrinkled his pointy nose, just like Anemonie always did.

Casper wondered how he'd not seen it before. *Those noses!* Who else but Blights would be so reckless with their belongings, so threatening with so little provocation?

Lamp shuffled up behind Casper and cleared his throat. "Casper," he whispered, "I've been doing some counting and I think we've got them outnumbered. I'll take the boy, you take Anemonie, I'll take the girl and you take the boy and the girl. Then I'll hold the rear and you watch for pigeons while I take Anemonie." Lamp grinned with pride at his tactics.

"Let's hold back on a battle for now, Lamp." He smiled at the three Blights, knowing full well they'd heard every word of Lamp's plan. "We're all friends here, eh? Any bad blood between the Blight family and us is just water under the bridge. Ain't that right, Anemonie?"

"Whatever, Candlewacks." She snatched a look

to see if her new cousins approved of her put-down.

Anemonie and the Blight visitors had already started up the road towards the park and Casper didn't want to get left behind – not this morning, anyway. There was no question about it – the village felt distinctly odd.

"Hey! Where are we going?" shouted Casper, scuttling to catch up.

"*We're* going to my house to laugh about the lower classes," sneered Anemonie. "You can waddle off home for all I care."

"No, no, cousin, what sort of courtesy is that?" Briar fixed a firm gaze on Anemonie and, for the first time in her life, she submitted. "We could at least offer them tea. They won't have had the pleasure of real scones before." He made *scones* rhyme with *bones*.

Lamp's face crumpled in confusion. "What's *scoenes*, then?" he said.

"It's what the well-bred eat in place of your, huh, *scons*." If Briar had said the word any more hatefully, scones everywhere would have risen up and revolted.

Lamp, however, didn't get the tone of voice and took it as a valid answer. "Oh," he said, nodding. "They sound rich."

"Shouldn't we take your car?" asked Casper, looking back at the smoking wreck outside Lamp's garage.

"Phh," spat Briar. "I've got loads more at home. Have it, if you like. Sell it. Looks like you could do with some new clothes."

Anemonie guffawed as if Briar had just told the

funniest joke since a chicken crossed a road, but Casper hadn't noticed one at all. Chrys chuckled along too.

"I'll have it," chirped Lamp. "I can use the windscreen wipers for my hamster submarine."

In the park, the slide and swings had disappeared, and Sandy Landscape's flowerbeds had been replaced by sludgy heaps of mud.

I don't understand, thought Casper. *We were only here this morning. What's happened?*

The feral pigeons had flocked after the group, perching on nearby trees and keeping their distance, but Casper could feel their beady eyes hungrily watching his progress.

Anemonie strode ahead purposefully. "I'll show you the family portraits and the torture chamber and the trophy cabinet. I'm the five-times Kobb

Heavyweight Champion, featherweight class, and I'm Miss Corne-on-the-Kobb twenty-twelve." She simpered at Briar. "See? Strong *and* pretty."

Casper remembered the Corne-on-the-Kobb beauty pageant like a bad, bruised dream. "Didn't you win that one by fighting too?" Anemonie had given all the other contestants black eyes, or worse, and won by default. Teresa Louncher was still growing back an ear.

"Shut up, Candlewacks. I won that pageant fair and square. Not my fault if the other girls bruise easily. Should'a worn more make-up. Face it, you're never gonna win any beauty pageants and you're just jealous. I'm pretty and you're ugly. I'm rich and you're poor. I'm everything and you're... uhh?"

She'd turned the corner to approach the grounds

of Blight Manor, took one look at her house and stopped, dumbstruck, scratching her pointy nose in confusion.

"Ah," said Briar, patting his distant cousin on her bony back. "Yes, sorry, old girl. We've… made a few changes."

Chrys snorted. "You can say that again."

This made no sense. Casper recognised the same old black stone manor house, crumbling and crooked, a holey slate roof and withered stone tower climbing wearily towards the clouds. But now from two sides shot an enormous perimeter fence rimmed with barbed wire, behind which Casper could see three long, depressing concrete warehouses belching black smoke from sooty chimneys, and two gigantic watchtowers stretching higher than the house. The warehouses were enormous, cutting through most of what was Kobb Wood, meeting the perimeter fence again as the hill began. To Casper's left, along Long Lost Drive, came a bubbling torrent of water down a wide concrete channel where the road had been. The channel bent left as it reached the drive of Blight Manor, narrowed and then swallowed the gurgling water underground just as it approached the perimeter fence.

This *was* Blight Manor, yet it *wasn't* Blight Manor. This *was* Corne-on-the-Kobb, yet it really *wasn't*. A pigeon landed on Lamp's head, ragged and wiry. Its eyes glinted black as it watched Casper, chipped beak cocked sideways.

"Briar, sorry, but… where are we?"

"Aha," Briar chuckled, turning to look Casper straight in the eyes. His nose wrinkled, his lips curled into the patronising grin only given by a teenager in a suit. "I think the question you meant to ask, Casper Candlewacks, was '*When* are we?'."

Lamp looked at his watch.

When. That one word sent a shiver of understanding down Casper's spine. *When are we?* Not the twenty-first century, that's for sure. But that meant… The Time Toaster… Had it worked after all?

"And if I did ask that question…" Casper's voice fluttered like a butterfly with wind. "What would the answer be?"

"Why," smiled Briar, "the year of our lady 2112, November, just before lunchtime."

"Lunchtime?" Lamp's ears pricked up. "That's my best time of all!"

Chapter 7

Man o' the Manor

"Master bedroom." Briar Blight swept into a luxurious velvet-clad room, complete with a four-poster bed.

But Casper had hardly noticed. *The future*, he kept saying to himself. *We're in the future.* He touched surfaces as he passed to see if they felt the same as in the present. Generally, they did. Leather felt a bit softer.

Lamp didn't seem to mind much that he was in the future, as long as he was getting lunch. Anemonie's jaw hadn't closed since she stepped inside the grand palace that she'd known as her home for the last twelve years, but which had never had so much as a carpet for furniture.

The tour was carried out with grandeur, pride and a little script that Briar kept hidden in the palm of his hand. "This room comes equipped with walk-in wardrobe, en-suite bathroom, en-suite television and twenty-four-hour en-suite maid service." When Briar pulled out a TV remote from his pocket and pressed the buttons for channel 114, a hatch in the ceiling flipped open and a blonde-haired woman about the age of Casper's mum tumbled out and landed on the floor.

"Cool!" breathed Anemonie, closing her jaw for the first time, and only because she was dribbling. "Still, mine's better."

The woman leapt to her feet and curtseyed. "Sorry m'lord. Came as fast as I could, m'lord." She curtseyed again.

"Maid, our guests need refreshment. I want cream tea for five in viewing gallery two."

"Yes, m'lord; sorry m'lord," gasped the woman, curtseying like crazy and brushing down her crumpled clothes.

"Well? Don't just stand there. Get to it, woman!"

"Yes, m'lord!" She curtseyed, dashed to the door, curtseyed again, closed the door as she left and then came in one more time to curtsey before slamming the door and sprinting away down the corridor.

"Who's that, then, and why did she do all that bouncing?" asked Lamp.

"She's staff," said Briar dismissively. "I assume you don't have any of your own."

Lamp scratched his head. "There's a swan who helps me with my laundry."

"I've got loads of servants!" shouted Anemonie. "They live downstairs and cook my chips. I mean… they did. I mean… they do, but not here. Well, here, yes, but not *now* here. *Then* here." Anemonie blinked hard and pretended she knew what she was talking about by nodding earnestly at Briar.

In all honesty, Casper was still about as confused as Anemonie. Here he stood in the future, taking a tour round a future house owned by a future boy and girl. The Time Toaster had worked after all. One hundred years had passed in the time it took to burn some bread. Of everything Lamp had invented, this outshone them all. It was incredible. Amazing. Too good to be true. Casper checked the floor once more to make sure it was still solid. He pinched the skin on his arm. It stung; this was no dream.

"Lamp," he hissed. "You're a genius."

"No, I'm a Lamp," said Lamp. "But my mum says if you rub me three times, a genius might come out."

"That's a genie," said Casper, "and... never mind."

"Come on, chaps," Briar clapped his hands. "Plenty more to see."

Chrys's room was tiny in comparison: smart, neat and fairly dark, without a maid in the ceiling.

The girl kept quiet for most of the tour, preferring to snarl and shuffle along behind everyone else. If she ever did speak it was to correct Briar's mistakes, and in those cases she'd get a dismissive nod or a clip round the ear.

The dining room was lavish and wood-panelled, the kitchen a buzz of activity as dozens of cooks prepared untold quantities of delectable dishes. The sitting room was a picture of luxury with velvet curtains and silken sofas, a flat-screen telly the size of Casper's house, and a fireplace complete with real fire.

"The only types of fuel we use are banknotes," Briar explained, tossing on a few hundred quid to stoke the flames. "They really are the least efficient. How wonderfully wasteful."

"Quite!" cackled Anemonie, sweeping up

the thirty or so pounds that had fluttered back into the room and stuffing them into her pockets.

"Onwards!" Everywhere Briar went he used his remote control to open doors, to flick on lights, to summon maids. He had a channel to turn the stairs into an escalator, a channel to turn his shoes into rollerblades and even one that played his bank statement via a tannoy system into every room of the house.

"I suppose you're wondering," said Briar, pointing his remote at a pair of grand French windows, "how I could afford all this." The windows swung open and Briar led the others through into a drab courtyard that led to the three warehouses. He swu   arm proudly about the view. "THIS is my   tune. My family fortune."

Briar winked at Anemonie. "*Our* fortune. Come, come."

They climbed a set of clangy metal steps that led up the side of the middle warehouse – all apart from Briar, that is, who had a servant to carry him up. At the touch of channel 782 a thick iron door flipped open, and Casper and the others walked through.

"Urgh!" The height was dizzying. Casper stood in a globe-shaped glass room that hung above the warehouse's interior. Beneath his feet, only a see-through floor stood in the way of a good fifteen-metre drop to ground level. Below, a factory floor throbbed with workers, busying about in white overalls. Casper swayed, nauseous, as he tried to swallow his fear of heights. "It's certainly… erm… high."

"The perfect place to watch my minions do their duty," announced Briar. "It brings a tear to my eye just to see it." He chuckled. "Not really, of course. I had my tear ducts removed when I was six. Crying is a weakness, and what do we say, Chrys?"

Chrys's lip curled. "Weakness is for the lower classes," she said.

"Too right it is. We Blights, we're the cream that rises to the top, the dog that gets the bone, the lion that eats the panda. We are strength!"

Casper stuck up his hand. "Lions don't eat pandas."

Briar exploded. "THEY WILL IF I TELL THEM TO!"

"Yes, sorry, yes." Casper backed away towards a glass wall.

"Anyway…" Briar took a deep breath and

his face returned to a normal colour. "There's a reason for my saying this. You see, for all those poor lower-class serfs around the world, we have a solution." A maid ran in carrying a silver tray, upon which stood five plastic bottles with navy blue labels, the words ESSENCE OF NOBILITY written on them in fine ivory letters.

"Take one," said Briar, "and drink. It's delicious."

Casper waited until Lamp had gulped down a mouthful of the clear liquid in his bottle before he took one himself. It tasted of water; slightly chalky with a hint of fish, but mostly just water.

"*Essence of Nobility*," Briar said grandly. He took a hefty glug and wiped his mouth with the back of his sleeve. "A little drop of nobility in every bottle. Pure filtered mineral water from the River Kobb, with a dash of my secret ingredient. Guaranteed to make you feel twenty per cent posher in twenty-eight days or your money back!*"

Casper heard the asterisk in Briar's tone of voice, but couldn't find any small print. He took another glug. It wasn't too bad, as water went. "So what's the secret ingredient?"

Briar smiled. "My spit."

Casper's mouthful splashed on to the glass floor. "Ack! That's disgusting!"

"I quite like it," said Lamp, and he took another gulp.

Anemonie, who'd not opened her bottle and was now glad of it, cackled. "Drop of nobility in every bottle? You sneaky sneaker. You're a true

Blight, Briar Blight."

"A true Blight I am, Gran… er… Anemonie. And as family, you can be part of this. In fact, I'm feeling kind today. You all can!"

Casper shared a look with Lamp. "Thanks, but we should really—"

WAANG. WAANG. WAANG. An ear-shattering alarm split the air with its screaminess.

Briar's smile froze on his face. His nose twitched.

"Escape?" muttered Chrys.

"YES, THANK YOU, CHRYS," he bellowed – then added quietly, "I know what it is, sweet sister. Now let's go and sort it out before someone gets hurt." His courteous smile returned as he faced his visitors. "Come," he said, "I've got something to show you. Mr Flannigan, I think you in particular will enjoy this."

The Blights rushed out and down the steps, followed by Casper, Lamp and Anemonie. Out in the courtyard the alarm *WAANG*ed even louder. Everywhere, guards with black hairdryers tore about, shouting orders at each other or themselves or anything that would listen. The flock of feral pigeons had settled on perimeter fences all round the compound.

Briar grabbed the nearest guard. "Where are the escapees?"

"Dunno, boss." The guard shrugged, cowering from Briar's grip. "Please don't hurt me."

Briar thought about it, but chose to let his grip loosen. "Find them. GO!"

"This way," he snapped to the others, hurrying back into Blight Manor.

Briar led them up two flights of stairs, along a tiny corridor and up into the tiny tower that poked out of Blight Manor's roof. The dusty room at the top had barely enough space for the five of them, but once Lamp had stopped dancing they could all squeeze inside. A large window faced down towards the redirected River Kobb that flowed into Blight Manor, and Casper could see a man in sopping white overalls climbing out of the water, dripping wet and tiny.

"There's the fool!" cried Briar. He drew his remote from a pocket, pointed it at the man, tapped in a three-digit channel and pressed PLAY.

Instantly the man collapsed to the ground, twitching and shaking like he'd been struck by lightning.

Casper gasped. "What are you doing?"

The smile on Briar's face was halfway to demonic. He held PLAY with a steady white finger, but beckoned Casper with the other hand towards the window. "Shh. Listen."

Casper did as he was told. Through the opening in the window, all the way down on the grass, Casper could hear strained bursts of... laughing. The man down there wasn't in pain, he was being...

"Tickled," said Briar, reading Casper's mind. "It's harmless. Just a little deterrent. They love it, actually, but you try running away while being tickled."

Four guards came sprinting from Blight Manor and launched themselves on top of the escapee, but his howls of laughter continued.

"You can stop now," muttered Chrys. "We've got him."

But Briar kept the button held down. "A little longer. I want him to remember this."

The guards could barely keep hold of the escapee as they carried him back, wriggling and giggling as he was. "Stop!" he yelled. "Too much! I can't!"

Eventually, once they'd disappeared into the building, Briar let go of the button and inspected his remote lovingly. "Tickle Tags. Invented by a friend of ours. Tap in a channel, activate the electronic bracelet round the employee's ankle, and, *bzzt!* It sends a tickling sensation round the wearer's entire body. Genius, I'd say."

Casper shivered. "Brutal, I'd say."

"Brilliant, I'd say," grinned Anemonie.

 "Sausages, I'd say," said Lamp, who'd sniffed lunch.

Chapter 8

Casper Gets a Job

Lunch was exquisite and ridiculously expensive. Once Briar had finished his caviar and ketchup he threw his gold-plated dinner plate to the gold-plated carpet, where it shattered into a hundred wasteful pieces. Then he wiped his mouth with a twenty-pound note, threw it over his shoulder and burped. At the press of channel 26 a maid came with a vacuum cleaner to gobble up the mess.

Casper had no interest in the mother-of-pearl-barley stew on his plate. He glanced over to Chrys, who picked away quietly at her hard-boiled dodo's egg (procured at great expense from Charles Darwin's private collection of extinct stuff).

"Everything you can see we've earned through hard work," announced Briar, even though nobody had asked. "I like to think back to when my granny started this company in olden times. Did even she know how successful it'd be?" He snatched a look at Anemonie, but she was busy tearing a roast quail apart with her teeth.

"Within two years she was shipping to sixteen countries, shifting one million units per month and having to hire her cousins to help out with all the spitting. Even the Queen was drinking *Essence of Nobility* to top up her poshness. Turned out everyone wanted a drop of Blight." Briar threw back his chair, stood up and walked to the fire. Quickly the maid returned with her vacuum cleaner and sucked up the chair, the rug and then the tablecloth. Casper and the others had to leap back as the silver tableware whooshed away from them.

"Now, you will retire to your rooms. Supper is at six."

Casper coughed. He didn't feel comfortable amidst all this wealth. "Sorry, Briar, but we really must be getting on."

"And where do you plan to go?"

"Erm…" With the Time Toaster out of commission and the village a hundred years out of time, Casper hadn't a clue. "We'll just wander."

"In these streets? With those pigeons? Bah!

Too dangerous. And anyway –" Briar extended his welcoming arms and pressed channel 51 to summon a clutch of butlers – "my home is your home. Whatever you need, it's within these four hundred walls." By the look Briar gave Casper, it was all too clear that the lad knew every detail of how they'd got here and, crucially, why they couldn't return.

"I'm staying." Anemonie had been mostly swallowed by an enormous comfy chair.

"Good. And the boys?"

Lamp was rolling on the floor with a bundle of kittens that he'd found in a basket marked KITTENS. "Say we can stay, Casper! I love kittens the best of all."

"You're too kind, Briar, but we mustn't put you out like that. We can stay at Bernie Biffin's Beds

& Burgers. It's only up the road." Casper grabbed a handful of Lamp's boiler suit and made to leave.

"You're out of touch, old boy. Bernie Biffin's burnt down years ago, and I had absolutely nothing to do with it. No, I won't have it. You must stay, or what sort of a host am I?"

Reluctantly, and only after the offer of a session in Briar's 5-D cinema (where you can actually *taste* the explosions), Casper agreed.

His room was smaller than he'd imagined and the bed was fairly lumpy. Obviously in the last hundred years breeze-block walls, bare light bulbs swinging from ceilings and wonky loos in the corner had become the latest fashion in interior design. Casper wasn't a massive fan, to be quite honest.

Through a grate in the wall, the sounds of Lamp getting comfy in his room next door could be heard. "Casper," Lamp moaned, "I can't jump on my bed if it's not bouncy."

Sounds of jumping were replaced by a *thonk* noise, which spelt the end of Lamp's attempts to soften the bed up.

"You all right?" asked Casper.

"Landed on the floor," said Lamp. "Can't feel my bottom."

Five minutes later, deep snores resonated through the grate.

I'll wake him up for supper, thought Casper. After all, it had been a long morning.

Casper shared the room with a line of ants and a noisy wasp at the window, but when he tried to let the wasp out, he found the window was locked.

"Looks like we're bunkmates," Casper said.

"*Buzz*," said the wasp predictably.

Casper had noticed on the way in that the number on his door read 34128. Lamp's was 34129, and other doors on his corridor held similar numbers like the rooms in a hotel. Blight Manor was obviously set up for a lot of guests, some more important than others. Perhaps Briar had given Casper and Lamp the wrong rooms.

The door of Casper's room was locked too. Security was quite tight here, and most of the important doors were opened with a handprint scanner, this one included.

Casper fitted his hand to the scanner, but after a few short seconds it flashed red. "I'm sorry," said a friendly robot voice, "your print has not been recognised. Please hang up and try again."

"I'm Casper Candlewacks," Casper said. "I'm a guest of Briar Blight. Can you go and get him? I think I've been given the wrong room."

"Sadly, I'm only a handprint scanner and am incapable of movement," the scanner said cheerily. "Otherwise I'd go right up there and talk to his lordship myself. In the meantime, would you like me to read your palms? Your longevity line looks particularly pronounced."

"You know what, I'm fine," said Casper, disappointed. "It's probably a mistake. I'll wait for Briar."

Casper shared a withering look with the wasp and lay down on his lumpy bed. Lamp had been right. A granite slab was bouncier than this mattress.

The afternoon dragged on in room 34128.

Casper realised he'd left his book at home and the only bits he could remember were the bits he'd already read, which was frustrating. He tried to wake Lamp up for a chat, but Lamp mistook Casper's voice through the grate for a ghost and hid under his bed. Briar never came back to show Casper to the 5-D cinema. He hadn't returned to offer them tea, either, and supper was looking less and less likely. Had Briar forgotten about them? Outside, the sun set and Casper's room filled with gloom.

The wasp stopped buzzing.

Lamp was snoring again.

The light bulb flickered out and Casper let his eyes droop. *I'll sort it out in the morning*, he thought, and then drifted off to sleep…

***

BZZT.

"Ooh!" Casper jolted awake and scratched his leg. It was morning, and by the feel of it the wasp was already up.

BZZT. BZZT.

"Stop it!" He sat up, scratching his arm and his neck. "If you're not careful you'll sting me!"

BZZT.

"OY!" The wasp was all over him now, tickling his knees and his armpit and the tip of his nose. But wherever Casper scratched, it just tickled more. And then a word resonated in Casper's head. *Tickled...*

With disbelief he reached down to his right ankle – and felt cold, hard plastic. All Casper could do was laugh. A white bracelet, sturdy and bleeping red, had been clipped to his leg. And over his jeans and T-shirt he wore a set of heavy grey overalls. He should've seen it coming.

BZZT.

"All right! *Bzzt!* I get it!" Casper bellowed to nobody, leaping up from his bed and shaking out his itching ankle. "I'm up. Better?"

The handprint scanner hummed into motion. "Good morning, employee 34128! And how are you today?"

Casper checked his ears for wax. "Employee *what*?"

"Please place your hand on the scanner and we'll sort you out with some breakfast."

Bewildered, Casper did so. After a moment it flashed green and the door swung open.

At the same moment, Lamp emerged, giggling, from his room, wearing the very same set of overalls Casper had, only a couple of sizes bigger. "Hello, Casper – OOH!" he cried, kicking his right leg upwards like a can-can dancer. "Someone's tickling me. I think it's a ghost. He was talking to me last n—EEH!" He jiggled around once more.

But as Casper waited for Lamp to calm down, doors up and down the corridor started to open. Then other people in the same grey overalls emerged from them, silent as mute buttons. Each one had a sullen, heavy frown and downcast eyes. The nearest, a gaunt young man with cropped brown hair and a depressed moustache, looked at Casper with a puzzled face.

"Morning," said Casper cheerily.

The man's eyes flitted to his feet and he shuffled off down the corridor, towards the door that led to the stairwell. Others filed away in the same direction.

Casper frowned. "Bit rude."

"Maybe he doesn't speak human," suggested Lamp. "'Scuse me," he said, grabbing the arm of a middle-aged lady, her cheeks ruddy as apples. "Where are you going?"

The lady's mouth twitched, her eyes bulged and she sped away without looking back.

The corridor emptied of all its grey residents except for Casper and Lamp.

"We have to find Briar." Casper found himself talking to Lamp in a

hushed tone. "Something odd's going
on and I'm sure it won't end well."

BZZT.

"Oy!" Casper shouted at the ceiling.
"I didn't even do anything."

BZZT.

"I'm going! I'm going!"

The boys danced after the workers,
clutching their bottoms. On the stairwell
they found themselves joining an endless
tide of grey people, all trudging soundlessly
downwards. Every unremarkable corridor led
to another unremarkable corridor. Windows
disappeared as dank whitewashed stairwells led
down and further down, and then up a bit, but then
down again. Eventually, the stairs emptied into an
enormous room with long steel tables set with

hundreds of bowls of porridge.

"Breakfast!" cried Lamp.

BZZT.

"Sorry," said Lamp.

Following the others' lead, Casper took his place at a bench in the middle of a long table. Lamp squeezed into a space that didn't exist between Casper and a podgy bearded man, starting a domino effect that ended up with a little granny falling off the end.

The porridge tasted of metal, and the spoons had holes in them. When Lamp asked for syrup, he received a full five seconds of *BZZT* that left him rolling on the floor giggling and covered in porridge, which was still, sadly, syrup-free.

Lamp was hungry enough to eat the porridge off his own overalls, so he did (as did the chubby bearded man who'd finished his already).

"Somewhere up there, the Blights are laughing into their bacon."

Lamp's face darkened. "I want to laugh into some bacon."

No guards were present in the dining room, but somebody was watching, because every time someone talked, coughed or chewed too loudly their Tickle Tag was set off and they tumbled backwards off their bench howling with laughter between desperate yelps of "No more!" or "Not there!".

And then a room-wide *BZZT* meant breakfast was over, so the workers jumped up from the benches and marched out towards a far door.

Once again, Casper and Lamp flowed downstream. This time the stairs led up into the light of a cloudy day, across the courtyard and through a large double door on to the factory floor of Warehouse 2.

Inside, the crowd filtered this way and that, taking up their stations at a panel of bleeping buttons or overlooking a conveyor belt.

"We're not supposed to be here," cried Casper, but nobody batted an eyelid.

A hush fell as the final few stragglers found their way to a free spot. Casper and Lamp stood idly in the middle of a clangy metal walkway, bewildered.

"I don't like this place," said Lamp. "Shall we have breakfast again?"

WAANG, WAANG, WAANG.

All heads whipped towards the main entrance, where three figures strutted inwards flanked by half a dozen burly guards.

"Morning, chaps!" shouted the one in the centre. "Sleep well?"

Casper's toes curled at the sound of this voice. "Briar…" he muttered.

In step with Briar Blight, smartly dressed in a dapper black suit, were his two female relations: Chrys on his left and Anemonie on his right. Both wore smart white blouses and fitted black jackets, with matching shiny black shoes that clacked threateningly on the metal walkway. They came to a halt a few metres in front of the boys.

"What are we doing here?" demanded Casper. "Is this what counts as a joke in the future?"

Briar's satisfied smile settled on Casper for only a moment, before flicking over to Lamp. "Three four one two nine, you're with me. We have something special to show you."

Lamp pulled a confused face and looked behind him, but nobody was there. "My name's called Lamp, not numbers."

A shadow of amusement passed across Anemonie's lips. "Not no more, it ain't." She pointed a sharpened finger at the tag on Lamp's overalls.

The same number as on Lamp's door – 34129.

Casper looked down at his own tag – 34128.

Lamp got halfway through explaining that he'd been given the wrong overalls when two bodyguards stomped forward and grabbed an elbow each, lifting him high into the air. He was still explaining when the Blights turned on their heels and strutted off down the walkway.

"Oy! Bring him back!" shouted Casper, but the Blights didn't seem to hear.

The last Casper saw of him as he was whisked away into the courtyard, was Lamp spelling the letters of his name out in the air with a grubby finger. "L-O-N-P," he said, "spells 'Lamp'. I could write it down for you. Actually, I probably couldn't." And then he was gone.

The doors slammed shut and Casper found the rest of the factory looking at him.

"What?" he challenged.

One of the workers, a toothy chap numbered 12748, handed him a box full of navy blue lids and pointed to an empty station by a conveyor belt.

Casper frowned. "Sorry, I'm not meant to be here…" He looked around, but there was nobody to help him. A hulking guard with a truncheon the size of a fully grown badger stepped forward threateningly.

"All right!" Casper cried, scuttling away to the conveyor belt. This was ridiculous. Next time Briar appeared Casper would confront him, but he might as well play along until that time. He didn't want another *BZZT* again anyway.

Casper's role on the factory floor was to screw the tops on bottles of *Essence of Nobility*. The conveyor belt carried the filled bottles over to Casper's station at a terrifying rate, and if he spilt a drop or fell behind, he'd get a *BZZT* so tickly it felt like his funny bone would drop off. The workers around him screwed tops at a dizzying pace, their fingers twizzling so fast that the lids practically melted on. Most of them could do two bottles at once, one with each hand, but a big proud chap with a BEST

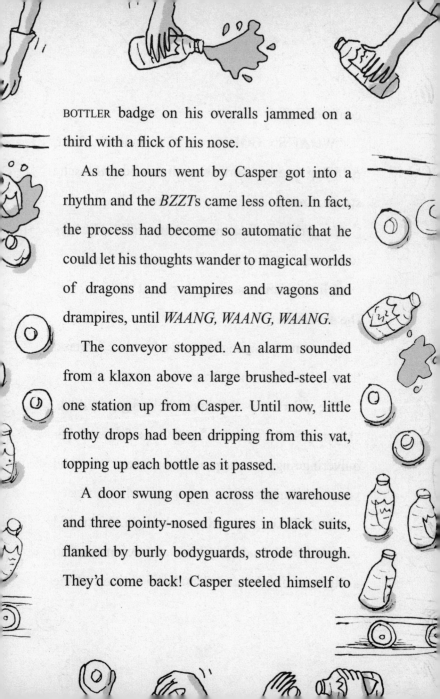

BOTTLER badge on his overalls jammed on a third with a flick of his nose.

As the hours went by Casper got into a rhythm and the *BZZTs* came less often. In fact, the process had become so automatic that he could let his thoughts wander to magical worlds of dragons and vampires and vagons and drampires, until *WAANG, WAANG, WAANG*.

The conveyor stopped. An alarm sounded from a klaxon above a large brushed-steel vat one station up from Casper. Until now, little frothy drops had been dripping from this vat, topping up each bottle as it passed.

A door swung open across the warehouse and three pointy-nosed figures in black suits, flanked by burly bodyguards, strode through. They'd come back! Casper steeled himself to confront Briar.

"WHAT'S GOING ON?" roared Briar, *BZZT*ing nearby workers with his remote as he strode through the factory.

Casper's heart beat faster. Anemonie and Chrys were with him, but there was no sign of Lamp.

A little woman stuck up her hand. "Please, sir," she squeaked.

The remote swung towards her and hovered there. "Yes?" snapped Briar.

The poor lady shivered like a shaved duck. "Umm, it's the spit vat." All eyes followed her quivering finger as she pointed upwards. "We need your… donations, sir."

"Ah," Briar said. "Good work." He turned on his heels, leading Chrys and Anemonie up a flight of metal stairs that led to the top of the vat, pointing over his shoulder to *BZZT* the little woman anyway.

The whole factory waited as the three Blights leant over the rails and got spitting. And my, oh my, what a lot of spit they had. Perhaps they'd been drinking milk, or maybe the upper classes just own super-productive salivary glands, but within five minutes they'd rained down pints of the stuff. Once or twice Anemonie 'missed', flobbing great gobs of goop over the side to land on the head of a worker.

Slowly, Casper melted away from his station and walked towards the bottom of the stairs. It'd be madness to confront the Blights up there. What with his Tickle Tag and the low metal rails he'd probably end up in the spit vat, and cleaning that stuff off his clothes would be less pleasant than camel burps. No, he'd wait for them to come down and then, calmly, sort something out. Casper still held a glimmer of an iota of a slice of hope that this was all a bad joke. Or maybe it was some big mistake. Perhaps one lucky worker had been given Casper's room by mistake, and woken up this morning in a golden bed with velvet sheets surrounded by performing monkeys and hand-peeled grapes. But most likely, one cruel word from Anemonie in Briar's ear had sentenced Casper to a lifetime of slavery in a factory in the future, producing bottles of watered-down spit. Yes, that sounded much more likely.

BZZT.

"YAHAHA!" Casper tumbled to the floor in a pile of giggles.

Briar put down his remote, took the stairs in

twos and stepped over Casper like he was a mangy dog. "Outta my way, slave."

"Yeah, slave," giggled Anemonie, who'd saved up one mouthful of spit for the back of Casper's head.

The three Blights strode away and the *BZZT*ing stopped, but Casper felt no less humiliated, lying there on the floor with the active ingredient in *Essence of Nobility* soaking into his hair.

Chrys shuffled behind the other two, snarling back at Casper, but at the click of Briar's fingers she was trotting to catch up again.

And then the conveyor whirred back into life and Casper found himself scrabbling to get back to his station before he could be given another *BZZT*.

Chapter 9

Blight Betrayal

That night, Lamp returned to his cell at what must have been close to midnight, collapsed on to his bed and fell asleep straight away. He was gone again before the round of *BZZT*s that woke Casper and the rest of his corridor.

Another day in the factory, then. Soon Casper settled into the routine: countless hours of bottle-topping with a ten-minute 'activities' break, where the activities on offer included running laps of the courtyard or getting a *BZZT*. Time was saved in the afternoon by providing lunch and dinner in the same sitting, in the same bowl. Today's lunch was rice, while dinner was rice. Great to have a variety.

In the evenings, locked up in his cell, Casper was encouraged to have some 'educational time'. Sitting on his chipped plasterboard bedside table was a fat book called *Blight – A History of Violence*, which listed every member of the Blight dynasty and the length of their noses. Lights-out never came soon enough, even though the nights that awaited Casper were cold, lumpy and full of bedbugs. Then – *BZZT!* – the morning tickle and an ominous threat of porridge followed, before it was time for work again.

Talking was forbidden, so making friends was

tricky unless you were one of those French mime artists, and Casper wasn't one of those French mime artists. But on the fourth day, or the fifth (or possibly the sixth – Casper was losing count), as he screwed the lid on his thousandth spitty bottle of the day, he saw the short, blond-haired boy to his right casting him a funny look.

"Hi," whispered Casper, before looking furtively around to see if he'd get a *BZZT*.

The boy (or 25227 as he was known) took a couple of screws of his bottle to decide if he'd answer back. When he did, it was hardly audible over the hum of the conveyor belt. "You… Casper?"

Casper nodded.

25227 gasped, took a step back and received a *BZZT* that made him squeak like a piglet and fall over. He got up without looking at Casper.

The whole exchange could only have taken ten seconds, but it confused Casper greatly. How did the boy know his name? Nobody within the factory had even spoken to Casper, let alone asked him who he was. But from then on, Casper noticed slight changes in how he was treated.

At breakfast, he would find people dropping an extra spoon of porridge from their bowl into his. 25227 and the other workers round Casper's station would bottle faster so that he could rest his wrists from time to time without getting a *BZZT*. When Casper grazed his knees after falling to the gravel during the activities break, the stocky bloke called 84192 gave him a piggy-back for the rest of the lap. Then the next day, kindly old 26057 handed him a bandage woven from pillow fabric when the guards weren't looking. It was nice that they'd help a total stranger, but Casper couldn't puzzle out why they'd bother. It was all a little baffling.

More baffling, though, was Warehouse 3. Warehouse 3 was off limits. Casper knew that from the enormous WAREHOUSE 3 IS OFF LIMITS sign painted on the front of Warehouse 3. But over the past few days, and increasingly often, Casper had been hearing booms and bangs, crashes and splats echoing from Warehouse 3's insides. Was that where they were keeping Lamp? And if so, what were they making him do?

The Blights rarely visited the factory floor, apart from the times when the spit vat ran dry. They had more important things to do, like counting their money and putting it in stacks. A little more often than he saw the other Blights, Casper saw Chrys sitting alone up in the glass pod above the factory floor. She'd sit for hours, watching the workers from on high with that nasty scowl of hers, like a lion watching a herd of antelope. Often she'd bring something to fiddle with, like a strip of bubble wrap or one of those squishy stress balls. Whether it was his imagination or not, Casper couldn't help feeling that Chrys was watching him in particular, though every time he looked up she'd be looking in another direction.

One night as Casper sat reading, the lights went out just as he was approaching his favourite page – the one about Lord Barrington III of Blight (1677–1748), who demanded that the whole of Britain be put to death after the local wine merchant ran out of good claret. Luckily, his messenger caught quite a few plagues on the carriage to London so when he got there, all boily and green, nobody took Lord Blight's order seriously.

With a sigh, Casper put his book away. It had been a long day. Well, all days were long in Warehouse 2, but this one had dragged on for ages. Like a leap day, or something. Sleep came easily, until suddenly –

Click.

Casper sat up with a start. Did he dream it?

Creeeek.

"H-hello?"

A soft voice rasped from a crack in his door. "Casper?"

It had been at least a week since Casper had last spoken. He tried to respond, but all that came out was, "*Gth?*" His mouth felt fluffy, and somebody's tongue kept getting in the way. He suspected it was his own.

The light flicked on, so blindingly bright that Casper had to cower under his scratchy blanket.

"Get your things. We're going."

"All I have is this book," said Casper. "Where are we going?"

"Out. Away from here. Whatever's in Warehouse three, it's… we need you out of here."

Nobody had even called him Casper for at least three weeks. He was more used to 34128. But someone had come to free him! Someone who knew his name! "Who are you?" He dared to peek out from behind his blanket.

There stood a girl in a pair of black pyjamas. She had a pointy nose, short spiky hair and a scowl…

Casper gasped and hid behind his blanket again. "Chrys? I-I'm so sorry." Why was *she* here? Surely she'd never free her own slaves?

"Shut up," said Chrys. "Get up, cos we haven't got long before it comes back on."

Nothing made sense. "We're… leaving?"

"Yes." Chrys's voice was cranky and curt. "Get up or I'll *bzzt* you."

"Sorry. Yes." Nodding wildly, Casper leapt out of bed and pulled on his overalls. He grabbed the only thing he owned – *Blight – A History of Violence* – and tiptoed out of the room after Chrys.

The corridor was as black as the inside of a box, but straight and narrow, so Casper could feel his way. When they reached the first staircase they went up, not down, up past two floors of identical dark corridors before reaching a large pair of double doors with one of those handprint scanners for a lock. Chrys pressed her hand on the outline and looked around nervously as the machine read it.

"Welcome, Lady Chrysanthemum," the cheery robot voice said. "And what lovely palms you have. Is that a new handcream?"

"No," she snapped. "Just let me through."

The doors swung open.

"It's cold out," sang the robot voice. "Did you bring gloves?"

Chrys didn't answer, pushing through the doors and out into the night air.

It is cold out here, thought Casper. He made a note to listen to robots in the future. The yard was deserted, which was just as well, because even if Casper told the guards he was sleepwalking, that was forbidden too. Chrys dashed through the shadows towards Warehouse 1 and Casper followed, terrified. They crossed the courtyard in no time, and with a handprint on the scanner and a quick chat about the weather, Lady Chrysanthemum had the steel doors open and was tugging Casper inside.

The sound of rushing water met Casper's ears.

"The River Kobb," said Lady Chrysanthemum. "In you go."

"Erm," Casper faltered.

"Don't be a sissy."

And then he felt a shove and the steel walkway wasn't holding his feet any more and he was falling and shouting, and then he was under the icy-cold depths and breathing was wet, and he'd dropped his book.

Swim against the flow, thought Casper. Behind him, the river gushed into the bottling plant and Warehouse 2. In front, at the other end of a blackened tunnel, there was a small patch of moonlight. Another splash from nearby told Casper that Chrys had joined him.

He kicked forward slowly, grabbing a breath at every stroke. Chrys swam faster, breathing less and making much better progress. Why was she helping? Was this some big trick? Would Briar and Anemonie be standing at the other end of the tunnel with the biggest *BZZT* imaginable to punish Casper's escape attempt?

Their splashes echoed and magnified into the inky blackness. Casper's legs and arms grew heavy as lead, but still they swam on.

The soft light of the moon glowed up ahead, growing larger every time Casper looked. But the tunnel was long, and the river was flowing in the wrong direction. Every metre he gained, the current instantly took half of it back.

WAANG WAANG WAANG.

"They've noticed!" glubbed Casper.

Ahead, Chrys hung on to a rung built into the side of the tunnel, waiting for Casper to catch up. "Just keep swimming."

The *WAANG*ing and the splashing filled Casper's ears, but it was getting brighter, and he could feel a breeze the next time he came up to breathe.

"Here. Climb out this side." Chrys had grabbed hold of a low root poking out from the left bank of the river.

Casper pulled himself out of the water, up the bank and instantly he could feel the chill of the night against his wet skin.

"We've got to run now."

"THERE THEY ARE!" A spotlight caught the two like rabbits in headlights.

Casper ignored Chrys's tugging and twisted round. The perimeter fence separated him from Blight Manor, the spotlight blaring from the top of a watchtower.

"We're out," he muttered.

"YOU COME BACK HERE, CHRYS." The roar, furious and bloodthirsty, came from Blight Manor itself. It was the voice of Lord Briar Blight. "YOU BRING HIM BACK."

Casper swallowed hard. This was no prank. This was an escape, a prison break, and Chrys had betrayed her brother.

"Hurry!" urged Chrys. "He's got spare batteries, we don't have long."

"RIGHT!" roared Briar. "FULL POWER. FEEL THIS ONE, CANDLEWACKS. RIGHT BETWEEN YOUR TOES. HA!— Oh."

Casper ran, cold and bewildered, across the lawn of Blight Manor. Briar should have *BZZT*ed him by now. Why was there no *BZZT*?

"WHAT'S WRONG WITH THIS THING? WHY WON'T IT…"

The trees thinned and Casper found himself turning right on to a street with tumbledown houses and the river flowing down the middle of the road.

"Keep running," said Chrys. "He'll send guards."

Back at the house, Briar was screaming with rage. "BATTERIES! SOMEONE BRING ME BATTERIES! I'LL GET YOU, CHRYS. YOU TRAITOR! YOU'RE NO BLIGHT. CURSE YOU! WHERE ARE THOSE BATTERIES?"

The sounds of the mansion faded into the distance until all he could hear was two sets of hard footsteps and the running water of the river. This road twisted to the left and brought them out in a large cobbled square, cut in half by the river that ran through its centre.

"I *know* this place," said Casper. "It's my village square. But it's so different."

A large stone building leant so far to the right that the rickety clock tower sprouting from its roof was almost sideways. The clock itself had a smashed face with the minute hand pointing outwards, on which three red-eyed pigeons perched. The other dark buildings that lined the square were in a similar state, all wrecked and abandoned. In fact the only thing in a good state was the huge, solid-gold statue in the centre depicting a proud, slim man wielding a bejewelled sword. He had the pointiest, longest nose Casper had ever seen, on which four pigeons were perching.

"My father," muttered Chrys. "Anemonie's son. Lord Oleander Blight. Horrible man. Come on, we're not safe yet." She set off for the far corner of the square.

They turned left, past a thick mud dam that had

redirected the river's flow on to the square, then left again down a wide stretch of road, then right on to a street of crumbling houses with a chipped sign that read CRACKLIN CRESCENT.

"I… I *live* here," Casper breathed. "Well… *lived*," he corrected.

Chrys ducked off the street at a familiar house on the left. Like all the others, it looked run-down and empty, but nevertheless she knocked three times on the door.

The letterbox flapped open and a pair of wide green eyes peeped out. "Who goes there?"

"Ahem. *The golden eagle flies at midnight*."

There was a pause. The eyes behind the letterbox blinked. "What time's it now, then?"

Chrys closed her eyes. "That's our password, Flanella."

"Oh, right. Our password." The eyes looked out at her two visitors. "Good. What do we do now?"

"You let us in," snapped Chrys, looking around for pursuers.

"How do I know it's you?"

"I gave you the right password, that's how."

"I didn't even know we had a password."

"*The golden eagle flies at midnight!* That was our password. Just let me in, they'll be on us any moment."

"OK, you may pass," said the eyes. The letterbox clanged as it dropped and everything went silent.

Chrys sighed. "Oh, for goodness' sake. Flanella?"

The eyes reappeared. "Yes?"

"Are you going to let us in or not?"

"Oh, yeah. I knew I forgot something."

The door swung open, Casper was pushed inside and the door slammed shut. Two smiling faces greeted him in the gloomy hallway. One was young, one old. One stood, one sat in a blooping, humming wheelchair. One was a stranger to Casper and the other was so very familiar.

"Hello, Cashper," grinned Betty Woons toothlessly.

"Hello, Betty," said Casper, hardly believing the words as they came out.

She held up a crumpled brown paper bag. "Jelly bean?"

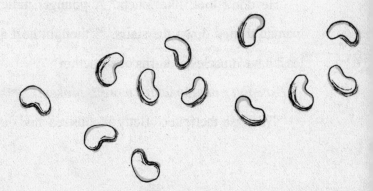

Chapter 10

The Unemployed

"This him?" The head of a chubby middle-aged lady poked out from the living room.

I'm home, he thought.

"He don't look like much." A younger, taller woman trotted down the stairs. "I thought he'd at least have muscles or horns or somethin'."

Except it's not home. It's more... broken.

"Thish ish the feller." Betty Woons reached out

her withered arm to give Casper a pat, her watery eyes twinkling. "Our little shaviour."

The ladies gasped and watched Casper adoringly, waiting for some sort of speech.

"Erm, hi." Casper smiled awkwardly. "I'm Casper. I used to live here. In the past, I guess. I'm not your saviour, though. And Betty… sorry, but how can you be here?"

The old woman looked no wrinklier than the morning at the bus stop, yet a hundred years had passed. She just winked knowingly and said, "I could ashk you the same question, Cashper."

"Lamp made a Time Toaster, and then we got imprisoned by the Blights. But Chrys freed me, and I don't know why she did that. I'm just a boy."

"That you are, Cashper," sang Betty wobbily. "An' a very speshal boy at that."

Apart from the cluster of grinning ladies standing in his hall, Casper's house hadn't changed that much in the last hundred years. There was still that faint smell of nappies. Casper's shoes stuck to the carpet just as they used to, and the same recognisable bite marks from his sister, Cuddles, still dotted the same wonky furniture. Mice still occupied the gap behind the floorboards, but judging by the two squeaking guards with tiny helmets protecting their hole, they'd developed considerably since Casper lived here.

"This is all very well, and thanks for bringing me home," Casper started, "but... can someone tell me what's going on?"

"Plenty of time for that." Betty waved her aged hands dismissively. "Come on, we'll get you out o' that tag." She whirled her wheelchair in a circle and barged straight through the other women using the plough attachment she'd fitted on the front. Hesitantly, Casper followed.

The ladies bustled after Casper, pushing him into a chair and rolling up the bottom of his overalls, lugging his leg on to another chair and inspecting the tag fearfully.

The young girl who'd been at the door, Flanella, galumphed away only to return with a thick black laptop computer, covered in wires of all colours, and various bleeping attachments. "Right then, Malcolm," she said, "let's see what you can do." She stretched one red wire straight, gave its end a twist and stuffed it into a gap in the links of

Casper's tag.

"I'm called Casper," said Casper. "Not Malcolm."

"I wasn't talking to you, then," said the girl. "Malcolm's my 'puter. He's helping me log into your tag. He needs the password, though."

The women looked at Chrys, but she just bit her lip. "Briar does that stuff. He never tells me passwords."

Flanella's face folded with concentration. "Ooh, I know!" she gasped. "*The eagle flies at midnight!*"

"No, that's *our* password," grunted Chrys.

"Is it?"

"Try… I dunno… try some of his favourite things."

Flanella tried PUPPIES, MARSHMALLOWS and CUDDLING, and then, under the instruction of Chrys,

MONEY, PAIN and SLAVERY.

As Flanella tapped away at Malcolm, Betty
Woons poured Casper a cup of tea-flavoured jelly
beans. He took a sip and chewed.

"There you go," warbled Betty. "Get them
down you. They're your favourite."

It was true. Back in the old days, 107-year-old
Betty used to give out packs of her home-made
jelly beans to all the kids in Corne-on-the-Kobb.
Some of them, like smoked salmon or hairclip 'n'
onion flavour, were yuckier than a cuddle with
a skunk. Casper would feed those ones to the
pigeons, saving pumpkin pie, toffee sundae and
his personal favourite, tea with two sugars, for
himself. It was nice to see Betty and her beans
again, even if she reminded him of home. Proper
home, that is.

Casper blinked. Something in his brain had gone *twang*. "Hang on, Betty…"

"Yesh? More tea?"

"Why are you here? I thought this was the future."

"Oh, erm, good point. I'd better go, then." She wheeled round to leave.

"Wait! Don't go! Tell me how you got here."

She braked. "I… erm… took the long way round."

"You mean you *aged*? But that makes you –" Casper did a quick mental calculation – "two hundred and seven!" She was wrinkly enough, but…

"Jelly beans an' strong brandy," she nodded. "Never mind none o' that fruit 'n' veg rubbish."

"Wow," breathed Casper. "Wish I could live that long."

Betty laughed at a joke Casper hadn't told. "You're doing all right, Cashper."

"I'm only eleven, though."

"You'll catch up," she said, and wheeled away to brew another pot.

Flanella had hacked into the tag by this time. (Turns out the password was PASSWORD.) She chatted away softly to Malcolm as she tapped on his keyboard. "Copy that folder," she'd say. "Disable data transfer, there's a good Malcolm." The wire attached to Casper's tag fizzed and gave him a little *bzzt*.

Casper winced. "I never got the hang of computers."

"'Puters are easy. It's just tapping or clicking.

Sometimes both. Malcolm's better than people because when you tap a person they don't do anything, just say 'Oy!' and tap you back. Also people don't have Wi-Fi. Malcolm does."

Casper hadn't a clue what the girl was talking about. He couldn't help thinking that out in the darkness of Corne-on-the-Kobb, Briar and his guards must be searching.

"Won't find us," said Chrys, reading Casper's mind. "I've been coming here for years. You've seen the front. Looks empty, like every other house."

"But what do you mean by 'here'? What are you all doing here?"

"We're the only ones left," said the chubby lady. "Our friends and families've been –" she shivered – "employed."

It hung in the air like one of Casper's baby sister's burps. Never had a single word seemed so ominous. Casper cast his mind back to the hundreds of workers inside Warehouse 2, and felt a little colder. "Those are your families?"

"Yer." The woman sniffed. "Ain't seen 'em for years. Maybe even months."

"But can't you rescue them, just like you rescued me?"

Chrys's lip curled. "You saw how hard it was just to get you out. Burnt my bridges now, anyway. Briar'll only have me back if I'm in more than one piece. You splashed too loud, Candlewacks."

"Sorry."

"Forget it."

He felt a bit guilty now. "So why'd you bother to rescue me if it was such a risk?"

"My brother's got your friend building something. He never let me see it, but you've heard the noises. Whatever it is, it's almost ready. And when it is, chances of escape will slip to just under none."

"But still, why rescue *me*?"

CLICK.

"Aha!" cheered Flanella. She hit the RETURN key with gusto and the tag unclipped, slipping off Casper's ankle like a suddenly bored snake.

Underneath, his skin was sweaty and pink. Casper scratched it with relief. "That's better, Flanella. Thanks."

"Me? No, it's Malcolm you need to thank."

"Oh… erm… thanks, Malcolm."

"Come upstairs, dear," said Betty. "There'sh a coupla people you'll wanna meet. They'll be able to explain things."

Casper helped Betty into a sturdy white stairlift.

"Ooh, be a love and push that green button."

Casper did as he was told and the stairlift ground into motion.

Half an hour later, they reached the top.

"Forgot me wheelchair," said Betty. "I'll just pop down in the lift an' get it."

"No!" shouted Casper. "No, it's fine. Let me get it."

"Shuch a gentleman," smiled Betty.

He trotted downstairs and hauled the wheelchair back up with him, then lugged Betty's frail frame off the lift and into its cushions.

"Thanksh, dear. You alwaysh were a good boy."

Casper finally thought to ask, "So who are we seeing?"

"I ain't seeing anyone. Just eshcorted you up here. First door on the right. Would you be a love and help me back into the lift? There'sh a good lad."

Casper sighed and transferred Betty into her lift. Then he took the wheelchair back downstairs where she'd be able to reach it when her stairlift got there. Betty gave him a wink as they passed on his way back up.

It was dark and silent upstairs, save for the grinding whirr of Betty's stairlift. Casper felt the need to tiptoe the length of the landing. He knocked on the first door on the right – his bedroom door – and waited.

"Enter," whispered an old, tired voice.

The door creaked like it always had. Inside, two decrepit men with barely any hair rocked gently on two rocking chairs. Casper edged forward, suddenly nervous. He held out a hand.

"Pleased to meet you, sirs."

"Better not," whispered the more slender of the gentlemen. "My companion here tells me that if I were to shake my own hand, the universe would explode."

"Your *own* hand?"

The gentleman grinned a grin that was bewilderingly familiar, and held out his hand for Casper to see.

Casper recognised that hand.

"Two freckles and a scar from the pigeons," the gentleman said. "Nice to meet me."

Casper looked at his own palm, and then up at the gentleman's face, and gasped.

Chapter 11

Know Thyself

"But… you're me!" cried Young Casper.

"As are you," chuckled Old Casper.

"Of course *I* am!" answered Young Casper.

"Well, we both are," answered Old Casper.

"What about me?" asked the stouter gentleman.

"No," croaked Old Casper. "You're not."

"Who am I, then?" The stouter gentleman looked confused.

"You're Lamp."

"Am I?" He groaned as he leant down to check the nametag on his sock. "So I am."

Young Casper stared wide-eyed at the old version of Lamp. "Look at your wrinkles!"

Lamp peered at Young Casper through the thickest pair of spectacles known to mankind. "Who's that, then?"

"That's me," said Old Casper.

"Is it?" The stouter gentleman took off his spectacles and gave them a wipe. "Have you cut your hair?"

"This is amazing," muttered Young Casper. "So you two must be… cor… a hundred and eleven? That's old."

Old Casper closed his eyes. "I remember saying that."

"Do you?"

"Oh yes. About a hundred years ago now."

"And sort of five seconds ago as well, I suppose," said Young Casper.

Old Casper nodded. "Oh, that too. I hope you're remembering all this."

"Why? Should I be?" Young Casper considered getting a pen.

"Of course you should. In a hundred years you'll have to say it all back to myself. I mean yourself. I mean… you get what I mean?"

"Not sure I do…" Young Casper scratched his head.

"Can we start again, please?" asked Lamp. "I've forgotten who I am."

"No, no, we can't start again. This only happened once, Lamp. I remember it as if it was yesterday.

But I suppose it's today…" Old Casper shifted in his chair. His face was wrinkled and so very pale, but his eyes still held that glint that Casper's mum loved so much. "Now, what did I say next? Ah yes, bloogle gargle Viking dromedary, please pass the pepper, Mildred, or I'll put you back in the fridge."

Young Casper was rapidly wishing he hadn't met himself. "Why did you say that?"

"Because I told me to."

"When?"

"Well, I'm just about to." Old Casper pointed to his wrinkled mouth. "You'd better say that all back to me, Casper."

"What, now?"

"No, no; give

it a hundred years. Don't want to rush things."

Young Casper had already forgotten the bit about the dromedary. "You didn't happen to write this conversation down, did you?"

"Oh yes, I gave me a transcript a hundred years ago." Old Casper tapped the pocket of his dressing gown. "I've got the whole conversation right here, in case I forget the words."

"Could I see it?"

"Not until afterwards. Wouldn't want you reading ahead. And anyway, I didn't give it to me until right after Lamp fell off his chair."

"But Lamp hasn't fallen off his chair."

"Not yet, no."

"I plan to," said Lamp.

"But if it's written down, then that means what I say is already set. What if I say something wrong?"

"You won't," assured Old Casper.

"How do you know I won't?" asked Young Casper.

"Because I didn't."

"Ah…" Young Casper didn't like that. "But I have free will. I choose to say what I want to say. Look… erm… *SOCK PUPPETS. GILGAMESH. FOTHERINGSWORTH PLEMM-PLAMM.* You can't have got all that written down."

Old Casper pulled out a dog-eared piece of paper and unfolded it. "Was that 'plemm-plamm' with two double ems?"

"Suppose so, yeah."

Old Casper replaced the paper in his pocket. "Thought so. Next, you'll say 'No, I won't.'"

"No, I won't." Young Casper clapped a hand over his mouth. "Oh, my goodness."

"Listen, Casper," said Old Casper, "we could do this all day, but there're only two pages left of the script. I've got to tell you about your mission."

Young Casper kept his mouth shut. No piece of paper was going to tell him what to say.

"Corne-on-the-Kobb is in peril," continued Old Casper in a wise, sage-like tone. "Over the past hundred years the power of the Blight family has exploded. It started with a bright young girl's business venture, and a few plucky kids pitching in to help. But she found success. Too much success, some say. She employed more of the village, and turned her house into a factory. Demand grew, and soon she was shipping her drink worldwide. Within twenty years, pretty much the whole village had enrolled at Blight Manor. Working hours were increased and pay was reduced." He paused.

"What are you waiting for?" asked Young Casper.

"Just for you to ask 'What are you waiting for?', and now you've done that, so I'll continue." Old Casper closed his eyes and continued to speak, more slowly now. "I'd had a taste of the future from, well, just now, actually. The people who listened to my story stayed unemployed. We're the lucky ones. But life has been tough and our numbers have dwindled. Power passed down through the Blight family, and now that tyrant, Briar Blight, has a stranglehold over the village. What was it now…" He took a peek at the script from his pocket. "Ah yes. He's using his slaves to produce his spit-water, while he takes all the profits. We both remember how bad the conditions were." He shivered. "The truth is, your family, your friends, the whole village, Casper…" His voice cracked, so he blew his nose on a handkerchief. "They're all slaves in that factory. It's your duty to free them. Liberate Corne-on-the-Kobb again; return it to its former glory and save the future."

Saving the future sounded epic. But it was what superheroes did, not eleven-year-old boys from Corne-on-the-Kobb. "Can you help me? I've never saved the future before."

"You'll work it out," smiled Old Casper. "It'll be tough, but you'll live to tell the tale. I am proof of that."

The younger Casper grinned.

Lamp awoke. "Ooh, have you finished? Can I…?"

"Yes, Lamp, go on," said Old Casper wearily.

With a grin, Lamp leant too far forward and his

chair rocked over, sending him toppling to the floor with an almighty thump.

Somebody came running up the stairs. She burst through the door. "Oh, Grandad, why do you keep doing that?"

"This is the most fun I can have given my bad hip, Flanella," Lamp said. "Would you mind picking me up?"

Old Casper folded up the script and leant towards Young Casper, his bones clicking wearily. "Keep that safe," he said, the effort of reaching out evident on his face. "You'll need it."

Flanella positioned Lamp on his chair, brushed him down and turned to the younger Casper. "Lottie Landscape's made you a bed out of earth and things. It's more of a flowerbed, really. But it's comfy enough and the worms won't bite. And you should sleep. Malcolm predicts it's a big day tomorrow."

As Casper left his room, he turned to say goodbye to himself, but he was already fast asleep and snoring like a warthog.

Chapter 12

The Legendary
Casper Candlewacks

The pigeons had already begun their scratchy dawn chorus when Casper finally got to sleep on his bed-shaped pile of earth, with its mossy pillow, on the floor of what used to be the laundry room. What with all the time taken up by escaping and swimming and remembering who he was and meeting his future self, it really was getting on for bedtime.

But just as he was settling into a really good dream about slaying goblins—

"GOOD MORNING!"

Casper groaned and rolled over. Standing above him was a slightly-earthy-on-one-side Flanella, proudly holding a big tray.

"I didn't know what breakfast you wanted, so I brung all of them."

Scraping some mud from his face, Casper sat up and received his tray. Flanella plonked herself down next to him.

There was cereal and muesli, black pudding, hard-boiled eggs and a cup of orange juice all on one plate, topped off by a dollop of golden syrup, a squeeze of ketchup and a raisin.

"Wow," said Casper, wishing he could go back

to slaying goblins. Tentatively, he took a forkful of black pudding dripping with syrup.

It was a surprising combination. Casper chewed thoughtfully and swallowed, washing it down with a spoonful of orange juice and ketchup that had pooled in the corner of his plate.

"Thanks," he said, putting down his spoon – desperately hungry, but aware that another mouthful might end in disaster.

Flanella grinned. "Did I do good? I'm trying to branch out from sandwiches."

"Oh," Casper said hopefully. "Are you good at sandwiches?"

"No. That's why I'm trying to branch out from them."

Casper set his tray aside. "So you're the granddaughter of Lamp Flannigan, eh?"

"Yeah," she said, with sadness in her eyes. "My mum 'n' dad 'n' gran 'n' uncle got rounded up, though."

"They're in Blight Manor?"

"Did you see them?" Flanella's face lit up.

"There were a lot of people in there. I didn't catch many names…" He thought it best not to tell Flanella why nobody told him their name.

"Oh. Anyway, if you're finished, we're ready outside."

"You are?"

"Yep! See you down there." She jumped up, ran out through the door, ran back in because the door in question was attached to a wardrobe, ran through a better door and disappeared downstairs.

Ten minutes later Casper emerged, blinking, into

his own back garden. Standing in a line wearing army camouflage and green berets were Chrys Blight, Flanella Flannigan, Betty Woons (in a camouflaged wheelchair) and the two other ladies – Andrea Snugglepuss and Lottie (short

for Allotment) Landscape. When they saw Casper they straightened up and saluted. (Flanella saluted a bit too hard and knocked herself out.)

"Oh…" said Casper, taken slightly aback by this display. "Can I… help?"

"Reporting for duty, SIR!" shouted Chrys, and they all saluted again (except for Flanella, who'd done enough saluting for one day).

There was quite a long pause while Casper worked out how to let them down gently. "I think you've… got the wrong idea."

"Of course we haven't," laughed Chrys. "You're Casper Candlewacks, right?"

"Umm, yeah," agreed Casper, wondering where this was going. "I think you've got the wrong Casper Candlewacks, then."

"Three-times saviour of Corne-on-the-Kobb, lifter of the Coriander Curse, bane of *Le Chat*, slayer of food critics, arch-nemesis of Anemonie Blight and bona-fide-time-travelling-freedom-warrior?"

"Not sure about that last one, but, yes, I have

travelled through time. But it was Lamp's m—"

"We've all heard the legends of your brave exploits," interrupted Chrys, "your fabulous adventures, your fair but often brutal vanquishing of evildoers. Briar has too. Didn't you see his face when you first introduced yourself? Why else would he want to keep such a warrior in his factories, where you couldn't harm him?"

"I think the stories might have been exaggerated a bit. I'm just a boy, really."

"Your coming has been foretold, Casper Candlewacks," said Chrys. "By yourself. Your older self, I mean. He mentioned it in conversation a few months back that you might pass by. And Betty's been reading her crystal jelly beans too."

Betty Woons did a couple of mystical hand wiggles to prove Chrys's point.

"'He will lead us into battle; he will crush our fetters and welcome in a new age of freedom,' they say. 'He is our salvation. He is our hope.'"

"He is our salvation," repeated the other four. "He is our hope."

"Briar Blight casts an evil shadow on this village. And now, with the help of my grandmother…" Chrys swallowed hatefully. "With the help of my grandmother, Anemonie Blight, Briar threatens to tighten his stranglehold even further. We must stop him with whatever powers we have. Well, here are our powers – a modest army, but a faithful one. I have risked everything to free you, and here you stand. We are here to serve you, Casper Candlewacks. You and you alone can free us. You alone can lead us to VICTORY!"

"VICTORY!" the other four cheered, and Betty

Woons let off a party popper.

Puffed and red-faced, Chrys nodded and retreated into the ranks.

Five shining faces looked at Casper, awaiting his first triumphant order.

He looked down at his feet, and then back up to his army. This was awkward. "Guys, I hate to disappoint you, but—"

A noise from behind Casper made him spin round. Standing by the back door, leaning heavily on withered hardwood sticks, were Old Casper and Old Lamp. Old Lamp stuck up both his thumbs at Young Casper, forgetting about his stick and clattering to the paving slabs.

Young Casper locked eyes with himself; the old one winked. Casper turned round to face his troops and repeated, "Guys, I hate to disappoint you, but –"

Chrys sighed. "I knew this was a mistake."

– "but this mission isn't going to be easy."

The girl's jaw dropped. Flanella grinned.

"We've got days of hard planning ahead of us, and I'm going to need everything from every single one of you for this to happen."

Casper's heart beat hard in his chest as he slung out orders left, right and centre.

"Chrys, I need to know everything you do about the layout of Blight Manor. I want its strengths, its weaknesses and the whereabouts of its bathrooms, in case anybody needs a wee mid-siege. Flanella, I need you to hack into and understand the workings of those Tickle Tags. If Briar can activate them remotely, Malcolm can deactivate them remotely. Andrea and Lottie: lookouts, weaponry salvage and reconnaissance. And Betty, fix me some jelly beans before my stomach caves in."

"YES, SIR." The troops stood (or sat) to attention, made a final salute and marched (or wheeled) off to do their duties.

Casper sighed. He'd never felt further away from home than at this very moment, and yet he was already there.

Chapter 13

Mission: Implausible

Three short flashes of the torch across Blight Manor's lawn meant Betty was ready. Casper replied with two flashes from his own, then nodded to Flanella. "It's time."

"Right, Malcolm," she whispered into the microphone bit of her laptop. "Remember what we practised?"

You know what they say: *Time flies when you're*

planning a siege. This could not have been more true than when applied to Casper's last three days. A blur of charts, plans and laps round the garden, all accompanied Casper's lingering feeling that he had absolutely no idea what he was doing. These people looked up to him, practically worshipped him at times. They treated Casper with the respect owed to a hero, to a legend. Funny what a hundred years could do to the collective memory of a village.

"He's ready," said Flanella. "Want me to press ENTER?"

"Fifteen minutes from when you do, yes?"

Flanella tapped Malcolm's keyboard, then nodded. "He says yes."

Casper looked round for Chrys, Lottie and Andrea, his three soldiers, hiding behind nearby trees. Each gave him a thumbs up. The time was now.

Casper gave Betty four flashes from his torch and hoped she'd not fallen asleep.

Thirty agonising seconds passed until he heard a noise. First a *VROOM-SPUT-SPUT* from Betty's position, then the cracking of branches and an engine's roar. The bushes across the lawn split in the middle as two headlights burst through them, skittering on to the lawn and screeching through a full circle before coming to a halt facing Blight Manor.

"HEY, LADDIE!" shrieked the ancient Betty Woons. Her aged vocal cords still had enough *oomph* to echo across Blight Manor's ramparts.

Three separate spotlights hummed into action and the old woman was suddenly blinking in pale harsh light, alone, in her wheelchair, in the middle of no-man's-land.

"Clear off, old woman!" came the reply from a high watchtower. "Want us to come down and employ you?"

"Ha!" screeched Betty. "You jes' try. I'm retired!" Her wheelchair roared again and the rockets fitted to its frame let out licks of yellow flame. The wheels skidded, tearing up the turf, then caught friction and propelled Betty straight towards Blight Manor at a furious pace.

The spotlights followed, confused. Casper heard laughs and a jeer from the nearest watchtower. But obviously none of these watchmen remembered what she was driving. You see, a wheelchair built by Lamp Flannigan does more than just trundle. The ridiculing taunts turned to shouts of alarm when Betty's wheelchair left the ground.

Casper grinned at Flanella. "Go for it."

At the tap of a button, Malcolm grumbled into action, his little fan whirring until he rocked on Flanella's lap. Malcolm would broadcast white noise, black noise and every other colour of noise on to every short-wave radio frequency for the duration of his battery life (about fifteen minutes). During this time, Flanella assured Casper that Briar's remote control would be useless, and the Tickle Tags just a clunky sort of ankle bracelet. When Malcolm's battery ran out, however, they'd be back to full operation. That gave Casper fifteen minutes, and not a second longer, to get the workers out.

In the few seconds that Casper had looked around, the scene on the lawn had changed dramatically. The three spotlights had split now, each one frantically picking arcs across the sky as they searched for Betty Woons. The manor was awake too, with guards on every tower and faces at the windows. The chug of Betty's engine hung in the air, growing closer and then dying, as she flew figures of eight over the building. Shouts arose as the wheelchair zipped through the sight of one spotlight, but by the time the other lights converged on that point Betty was long gone.

The distraction was in place. With everybody looking up, Casper had his chance.

He, Chrys, Lottie and Andrea leapt from their hiding places and scrabbled down the bank to the redirected River Kobb. Casper felt the ice-cold water seep through his army jacket to his skin, sapping the heat from his body. But this was no time to complain. He had a mission to do, and the three ladies following him must only see his best side. Casper plopped underwater to swim a few silent strokes, checking at each breath that the others were still following.

Betty descended for a shrieking fly-by, never coming low enough to risk her companions being seen. With no weapons save a handful of particularly spicy chilli jelly beans to throw at her enemies, Betty had already resorted to making the *RATTATATATAT* noise of a machine gun with her clacky old teeth. It seemed to be working, though. The last sight Casper saw before he was engulfed by the darkness of the tunnel was three watchtower guards screaming "LIVE FIRE!" and diving for cover.

Swimming downstream was easier than up. Casper was hardly out of breath before the cavernous Warehouse 1 opened before him. On the left was a stout iron ladder, which he caught hold of with one hand as the current swept him past.

Dripping, half frozen, but unobserved, Casper counted the other three up the ladder and made for the exit.

Chrys approached the handprint by the door with her usual scowl. This was the moment of truth – the only thing they'd had to leave to chance. Chrys laid her hand on the outline and scrunched up her eyes.

"Welcome, Lady Chrysanthemum Blight," said the handprint scanner. "Your hands are wet. Been swimming?"

Chrys sighed, relieved, but no less irritated than usual. "Doors, please."

"Well, don't mind me," sang the doors as they swung open. "A little small talk never hurts, my motherboard always said."

The courtyard was aflutter with guards and their guns, but they were all making their way up to the battlements. In fact, none batted an eyelid at the four figures prancing from shadow to shadow.

Chrys was equally short with the door into the sleeping quarters, but it swung open just the same.

Stairs swept downwards, leading to darkened corridors on each side, and Casper's memories of being 34128 flooded back. His head swam and he had to lean on the wall for support.

Chrys grunted. "Whenever you're ready, Casper," she said pointedly.

"Hang on." Casper closed his eyes and focused on breathing. "Just having a moment."

"Make it a short moment," said Chrys, making a sour face as she looked at her watch. "Eleven minutes till Tickle Time." She turned to face the door and placed her hand on the pad once more.

"Leaving so soon?" asked the cheery robot voice.

Chrys clicked impatiently. "Open all the employees' bedroom doors."

"Midnight feast, is it?"

"Just do it," Chrys grunted.

"No problemo," sang the handprint scanner, and hundreds of soft creaks seeped up from the stairwell.

Casper swallowed down the memories of spit and bottles. There were hundreds of prisoners,

Lamp included, sleeping in these quarters. Now was his chance to free them.

Lottie and Andrea split up to take a corridor each on the first basement floor; Casper and Chrys continued to the second, taking their own corridors here.

"WAKE UP!" shouted Casper, poking his head into each room in turn, flipping on the light and checking for movement.

"What is it?" one man grumbled. He saw Casper at his door and blinked. "Who are you?"

"No time to explain. Just get your overalls on and meet me in the corridor. We're leaving."

The first thing the man did was to fumble for his copy of *Blight – A History of Violence*, just as Casper had.

Casper continued down the corridor, awakening

each employee in turn with shouts, shakes or threats of tickling.

One room was empty. He looked at the number on the door: 34128. Casper shuddered, shook it off and moved on to the next room. Sitting upright on the side of his bed, rubbing his sleepy eyes and still filling the room with the lingering smell of cabbage, the wiry young man called 14307 looked up as Casper entered and let his jaw drop. "Three four one two eight!" he cried. "You've returned!"

"It's Casper, and I'm not staying. You're coming with me."

"Coming with you… where?"

"Outside."

Fear filled 14307's eyes. "But the tags…"

"It's OK. We've got a plan. Meet you in the corridor." And then Casper was out and into the next room, waking up the next escapee. And the next, and the next...

Precious minutes were passing and Casper still hadn't cleared his second corridor. "How many more of these are there?" he asked Chrys as they passed on the stairwell.

"Sixteen corridors. That's four each."

Casper looked at his watch and winced. Seven minutes left.

It took time, waking tired workers up. They'd roll over or fall asleep as soon as Casper had gone. One chap thought this whole thing was a dream. When he led his last corridor of employees to the top stairwell, his watch gave him just three minutes before Tickle Time.

"Out!" he shouted, ushering the endless ranks of grey-overalled workers into the courtyard. The guards were too busy on the ramparts with Betty Woons and her flying wheelchair to notice a thing.

The employees tottered in a wobbly line across to the warehouse, where Chrys counted them in and shoved them towards the river channel. The final few stragglers had hurried out through the cheery door, but worryingly, Casper had not seen Lamp among them.

Perhaps I missed him, Casper thought. *Maybe he's cut his hair since we last met, or I was helping one of the older ones down the step.* But Casper knew deep down this wasn't the case. He'd been watching closely for his friend.

The courtyard was free of employees now, and the chorus of yelps and splashing from below told Casper they were learning to swim. Casper performed a running bomb into the water, bringing

up the rear of this odd procession. Two minutes. This was going to be close.

At the end of the tunnel, Lottie, Chrys and Andrea were pulling the sopping employees out of the river.

"Run!" they shouted, pointing in the direction of the town centre. "Go! That way!"

They did as they were told, tripping over each other's legs to scramble across the lawn. Above, Betty's wheelchair still soared in screeching laps, but now two of the spotlights were dancing across the grass, picking out the scores of sprinting employees.

WAANG, WAANG, WAANG, came the siren.

The slowest swimmers had now emerged from the tunnel, but there was barely a minute left to climb up the bank and dash for safety. Up in the battlements there were shouts of frustration as Tickle Tags failed to activate. But Briar's voice could not be heard.

Where was he? Surely the clamour of the escape sirens had woken him up, and Casper knew that if there were tags needing tickling, Briar would be the first to press that button.

Thirty seconds. The fastest escapees had cleared the lawn now, but many more were still scrabbling away across the grass, dodging spotlights and bumping into the occasional tree.

A cacophonous screech of metal on metal tore through the air from inside the Blight facility, so ferocious that everyone, escapees and

spotlight operators, stopped and turned to face its source. It shook the ground, sending Casper to his knees. Around him, faces turned white.

"Warehouse three..." muttered one.

"RUN!" bellowed Casper to the escapees. "Get out of range! The Tickle Tag'll be up in twenty seconds! Just run!"

But they didn't. Everyone just watched. Shaking spotlights converged on the corrugated iron roof of Warehouse 3, which had started to shudder. The guards were as frightened as the escapees, and that frightened Casper even more than both of them put together. Slowly, the roof parted in the middle and the two sides folded outwards like an enormous toy box. Another screech came from inside, so tremendous that Casper turned away.

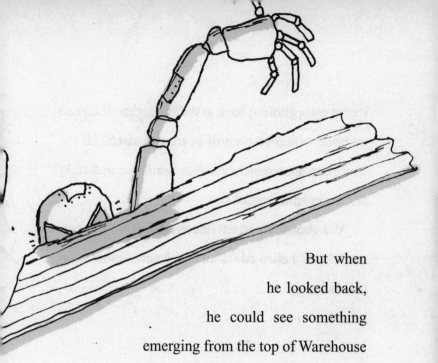

But when
he looked back,
he could see something
emerging from the top of Warehouse
3: a steel arm, as big and red as a bus, reaching
out into the night sky with searching clawed chrome
fingers. It found a sturdy bit of corrugated iron
roof and tightened its grip, crumpling the metal
like paper. Another arm reached up and grabbed
the other side of the roof, and then, like a granny
lifting herself from a bathtub, the arms tightened
and a demonic steel head rose from the warehouse,

its red eyes glinting back at the spotlights. It turned its neck with a screech of gears and stared all the way across the courtyard, over the fence and right at Casper Candlewacks.

And then Casper saw the robot's pointy, three-metre aluminium nose, and he knew his mission had failed.

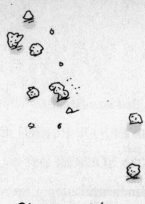

Chapter 14

Sweeping Up the Crumbs

Screams rang out from escapees and guards alike. Some started to run, but it was too late. At full height the robot stood twice as high as the tallest tower on Blight Manor. With jet-black spikes down its back in place of hair and the squint of its glowing eyes, not to mention its nose, there was no doubting its similarity to Anemonie Blight. But its voice, well, that was Briar.

"EMPLOYEES OF BLIGHT ENTERPRISES, GET BACK IN YOUR BEDS."

With one monstrous stomp, the robot had cleared the perimeter fence and was already catching up with the straggling escapees. Casper grabbed the arms of two older ladies and sprinted for the safety of Long Lost Drive. But he looked back in time to see one of the robot's hands point at an overweight man with short legs. A spurt of breadcrumbs shot from the thumb, covering the man and the grass around him.

As predictably as night following day, the pigeons descended. Clouds of them flocked from every tree, far more than Casper had ever seen before, squawking their hungry cries and flexing their talons.

The robot's hand swung to the next runner, and the next, scoring perfect hits with each as the seemingly endless supply of bread burst from its hand.

"Just run!" shouted Casper. "They can't get us all!" But then his watch alarm went *beep beep*, and he was no longer sure that he was right.

All around him, employees buckled to the ground, giggling, as the Tickle Tags began to activate. The two women he'd been guiding were now skidding along on the grass behind him like stubborn puppies, twitching this way and that with tears in their eyes.

The robot stormed forward, blasting every escapee who'd collapsed into tickling fits. With each additional bread-pile, new pigeons swooped down from perches, or old ones popped across from another course, engulfing their targets and pecking away at their bready bits. The two women slipped from Casper's grasp and moments later were covered in bread, then moments after that, pigeons.

Then the front doors of Blight Manor swung open and guards poured out to lug their tickled escapees back within its walls. The helpless workers cackled and slammed their fists as, one by one, they were dragged back into captivity.

With nothing left to save except his own freedom, Casper sprinted through the cackling crowds, only ever a few paces ahead of the robot's range. The escapees were a lost cause, he knew. Anyone with a Tickle Tag, no matter how far into town they'd got, would be as easy to recapture as a runaway tortoise.

Casper dashed through the park and its giggling hordes, who were yet to be breaded, but were in no state to run. These ticklees thinned out by Feete Street, and once Casper turned left into Cracklin Crescent he was alone again, the sounds of tickling and pigeons still hot in his ears.

The door was unlocked, the ground floor empty. Who could tell if the others would make it back at all? Casper stomped up the stairs, leapt the length of the landing and burst through his bedroom door.

"You knew!" he shouted, pointing an accusing finger at himself.

Old Casper awoke with a snort, then saw his visitor and nodded solemnly. "I knew, all right."

"Then why didn't you stop me? It was a massacre out there! Pigeons and tickling and that GIANT ROBOT! How could you omit to mention the giant robot?"

Old Casper sighed. "Because it happened, Casper. You can't change what's already happened."

"It hadn't already happened for me! Who did we lose? Is Flanella OK?"

"Miss Flannigan is fine, Casper, as is Miss Blight."

Just then they heard the sputtering sound of Betty's wheelchair engine and then a *swish* and a *crack* as she landed in the tree in Casper's garden. "And Mrs Woons will be all better after a few brandied jelly beans."

That was half a relief, at least. "And the others?"

"… are lost, for now."

Old Lamp grinned his toothless grin. "I made the arms out of buses, Casper."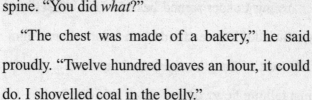

A shiver rose up Young Casper's spine. "You did *what*?"

"The chest was made of a bakery," he said proudly. "Twelve hundred loaves an hour, it could do. I shovelled coal in the belly."

"That was your invention?" Young Casper didn't know where to put himself. "You built that robot?"

"Yes," said Old Lamp. "Did it look good?"

Young Casper's throat made a *GACK* noise.

"He had to," interjected Old Casper with a withered nod. "That Briar fellow made you do it, didn't he, Lamp."

"Oh yes," nodded Old Lamp, his eyes going

misty. "I wanted to make a rollercoaster for bunnies. Course, I did make that, but twenty years later. And what a hit it was…" Lamp's gabblings continued, but more quietly and mainly to himself.

Young Casper turned back to face himself and grimaced. "I understand. And I don't blame him. This sort of thing has happened before. But, please, just tell me how you got out of this one."

Old Casper shook his head so solemnly. "No; this one you'll have to work out all by yourself. I really would help, but…" and then his head drooped and he let out a gigantic snore. A crumpled script, just like the one before, dropped from his hand, the last line holding one unfinished sentence. 'I really would help, but…"

Young Casper was on his own from now on.

Betty was downstairs at the kitchen table,

steadying her nerves with a handful of strong-fumed jelly beans from her '18s and over' collection. She'd managed to clamber her way into the spare wheelchair, a boring one made from the same thing you used to make baskets, with no rocket engines or anything cool. Casper joined her at the table, shared a sigh, then had a read through the script he'd have to memorise over the next hundred years.

It was funny to read his own speech written down. All the sentences were quite short and he used fewer clever words than he would've liked. Casper decided he'd try to sound cleverer from now on, slipping scorchers like *antiprofrogniloficate* into conversation as often as he could.

When he reached the script's end, he found a blank sheet of paper, less crumpled than the rest, at the back. He took it and laid it on the table, folding the other sheets back into his pocket.

"Why's this one here?" he asked, more to himself than to Betty.

"For your thoughts, Cashper." She leant over and tapped a white finger on Casper's forehead. "What'sh on yer mind, there?"

One thing in particular was on Casper's mind. "That stupid Time Toaster. If Lamp had never invented it, we wouldn't be in this mess."

Betty clicked her false teeth. "Yeh'll feel a lot better once yeh've got it out. Write it down, Cashper."

"Guess I could…" So he picked up a pencil and wrote:

Why the Time Toaster Should
Never Have Been Invented
by Lamp Flannigan

Casper found out the date from Betty, and added
that below –

18 November 2112

A boy who can't tie his own shoelaces should
not be a master of time and space.

I think we might have set in place the
downfall of Corne-on-the-Kobb, by giving
Briar Blight his evil grandmother and the
world's most gullible inventor.

Lamp Flannigan is my friend, but
sometimes when he does things like building
giant robots, I feel angry towards him, even

though it's not his fault.

I don't like that.

I don't even like toast that much.

Casper put down his pencil and read it back. Betty was right, he did feel a little better.

Betty read it over his shoulder. "Finished?"

"Yeah. Thanks, Betty. I do feel a little better."

"Heh, no problem!" Then she picked up the pencil, snatched the paper from the table, rocketed over to the other side of the kitchen and slammed it down into the toaster, before finally pulling the lever and grinning.

Casper looked on, bewildered, as the paper burst into flames. "What on earth was that for?"

Betty popped a jelly bean in her mouth and sucked gleefully. "'Bout a hundred years ago, your friend Lamp's about to be gettin' some toasht."

The old woman had gone barmy. "What's that got to do with you burning my paper?"

"Cor, do I 'ave to do all the work for yeh? The Time Toashter gets toasht from all acrosh time," she said dreamily, waving her wrinkly arm above her head. "Jusht so happensh that the piece of toasht it's about to get ain't a piece of toasht at all. It's a piece of paper. *That* piece of paper."

By the look of Betty's excited grin, Casper knew he should be remembering something. And then it came to him. "The article," he said, his brain working overtime, "the one we got from the Time Toaster back in Lamp's garage. '*By Lamp Flannigan*', it said. We thought that meant Lamp wrote it. But the paper was burnt, all covered in flecks of ash…" Casper thought back to the title of the note he'd just written. *Why the Time Toaster Should Never Have Been Invented* by Lamp Flannigan. "His name was just part of the title!"

Betty grinned. "And it made yer come 'ere, didn't it?"

"Yeah. After that message, we knew Lamp was on to something. But…" Casper took a long blink. Time travel wasn't his best subject. "How did you know to toast that article?"

"It's all circular, like the wheels of me chair," sighed Betty.

Casper was mid-headache when Chrys and Flanella burst through the front door, alive, un-breaded, but without Lottie or Andrea.

"They got them," grunted Chrys.

Malcolm let out a bloop of disappointment from under Flanella's arm.

"Just the four of us left. Hope you've got a plan, Casper."

He didn't. He had a headache.

Then Betty opened a cupboard, pulled out a second toaster, wheeled over to the table and plonked it in front of Casper.

There was an alarm clock strapped to the front of the toaster and dozens of watch faces boinging around on little springs. Casper had hardly finished his last gasp, before it was long past time for another one. "The Time Toaster! But it melted…"

Betty popped in another jelly bean. "You got work to do, Cashper."

Chapter 15

The Time Toaster Flies Again

"Why does everyone seem to know what's going on around here except for me?" cried Casper, exasperated.

Flanella stuck up a podgy hand. "I don't."

"Me neither," snarled Chrys.

Betty had pottered away into the garden to pick up the pieces of her wheelchair, leaving the other three sitting round the kitchen table, looking at the Time Toaster.

"We can assume Betty wants us to use it," said Casper, nodding to himself at every logical step, "and that she had a Time Toaster saved up for this very occasion."

"Can I just say…" Flanella chipped in, "erm… what's a Time Toaster?"

Casper explained for the third time.

"Cool…" Flanella licked her lips. "Useful for when you want toast."

"But what do *we* need it for?" said Casper, desperate to get back to the point.

"Escape?" mused Chrys. "Maybe she knows we've lost, so it's time to scram."

"No," Casper bit his lip. "Not Betty. She's no coward, and at her age she's got nothing to lose."

"Then it's got to be a way to help us defeat Briar and his stupid robot." Chrys scratched her head. "Maybe we're s'posed to send it back in time."

"If we send it back in time, wherever we send it, it'll cause havoc. And, anyway, I don't remember reading about a giant robot in any history books. No, we've got to take that mechanical monstrosity down here and now."

They thought for a while about that, then Flanella asked what a Time Toaster was again. Casper got her to write it down on Malcolm so she wouldn't forget.

Casper tried a new approach: listing all the ways you could take down a giant robot. Chrys suggested napalm strikes and precision nukes, which wasn't helpful because they hadn't got either. Casper thought that they could build another giant robot, and the two might fall in love and stop all the fighting, but Flanella said Malcolm didn't know how to build robots.

Finally, Flanella said, "Shame the robot's ankles aren't a bit thinner."

Casper frowned. "Why does that matter?"

"We could've fitted a Tickle Tag on it. Made it go all tickly and fall over."

"But those things were designed to work on humans."

"Malcolm says the tickle is an electrical signal. Malcolm says metal is a good conductor." She blinked. "But I don't know what that means."

"So what you're saying is, if we could get a Tickle Tag round the robot's ankle, and if Briar set the tickle signal off, it could work on the robot as it does on a person?"

Flanella tapped away at Malcolm for a few seconds. "He says yes."

"That'd be perfect! Just like with the workers, a Tickle Tag would immobilise the robot! And we've even got one spare after you took mine off."

The Tickle Tag lay limp on the table, white with metal buckles. Was it as simple as just clipping it to the robot? No. "You're right, though. We'd have to fit it round the robot's ankle, but it's far too small." Casper sighed. Another dead end.

After some more tapping, Flanella said, "Actually, best place for the Tickle Tag would be somewhere inside it. Where there's no armour and just pure squiggly circuit bits."

Chrys hadn't had much practice looking impressed, but she gave it a good go. "So all we've got to do is get inside the robot and you can do your work?"

"That's a problem in itself," groaned Casper. "We can't just slip down its throat."

"Oh, Malcolm got some snaps," piped up Flanella. She brought up a series of photos of tonight's assault on her screen, slowly increasing in mayhem to the point where guards flooded out to reclaim the workers and she'd had to run. One picture particularly interested Casper, though.

"What's that?" he asked, pointing to a mark on the robot's backside.

"Could you zoom in, please, Malcolm?"

Malcolm zoomed in, close enough to show a small door cut into the robot's casing with a little wooden doorknob. Some sort of goods entrance or something. Surely it was large enough for a Casper-sized boy to crawl through?

Casper took an excited intake of breath. "We could climb in there. Set up the Tickle Tag in a batch of juicy circuits and get out before Briar and Anemonie notice a thing. All we need is a distraction, and Betty's wheelchair did a pretty good job tonigh— Oh." Casper's plan came crashing about him like a house made of peanut butter.

Chrys snarled. She'd seen the problem too.

"Betty's wheelchair is no better than trash now," said Casper, through gritted teeth. "Aside from her, and with Lottie and Andrea, ahem, 'employed', there're only three of us. How are we supposed to bring out the robot AND distract it enough to climb inside its bowels?"

"We need an army," said Chrys.

And then Casper looked down at the Time

Toaster, and he knew what to do.

They took the back way to the bus stop, leaping over three different garden walls and wading through a fishpond to avoid the exposed walk along Feete Street. The bus stop stood alone on the side of the road, the wires still hanging from the timetable as Lamp had left them. With a bit of guesswork, a screwdriver and a couple of trial runs, the Time Toaster was ready to fly once more.

"Ready?" winced Casper.

"Sorry," said Flanella. "Erm… what're we doing?"

"You're about to see for yourself." He tapped in a familiar date on the buttons and cried, "*Let's TIME!*"

(Right. The next bit gets slightly confusing

unless you know when everything happened. So I'll add the dates and times, just to help you out. Thank me later.)

21 October 2012, long after dinnertime

Amanda Candlewacks was frankly livid when her son burst through the door.

"Casper Graham Ziggy Candlewacks, where on earth have you been?" she demanded, hands on hips. "You're late for supper. Yesterday's supper. I haven't seen you since the bus shelter thing."

Two cold bowls of baked beans sat next to each other on the kitchen table.

"Sorry, Mum. I've been… actually, you'd never believe me."

Two girls stood behind Amanda's son, both feasting their eyes on their surroundings as if this house were the Palace of Versailles. Amanda felt her heart race, and then her cheeks and the tip of her nose go red. Did Casper have… *girlfriends*? Two of them? "Oh… " squeaked Amanda. "Are these your friends?"

"Love what you've done with the place," said a sharp-faced girl who looked awfully like that Anemonie Blight. Amanda couldn't tell if the girl was being sarcastic, so she replied, "We're due for a redecoration. I was going to get a man in."

"NYA!" From her high chair in the corner, little Cuddles, Casper's sister, was getting bored. And with teeth like that, boredom meant bite marks.

Both Amanda's and Casper's eyes settled on the baby.

"Mum, can I take her for a while?"

Amanda frowned. The last time Casper needed Cuddles, it was to bite through a padlock that Lamp Flannigan had fastened round his wrist. "How long d'you need her for?"

"I'll bring her back before morning. You go to sleep."

"Ooh, that does sound nice. Haven't had a good night of sleep since three weeksmmm…" And then Amanda found her eyes drooping and her legs buckling, and Casper and his girlfriends were already halfway out of the front door with Cuddles slung under one arm.

5 June 1915, shortly after breakfast

The 1st Kobb battalion stood smartly to attention in the square, their bayonets fitted with those sharp

pointy sausages you get for a barbecue.

Crowds waving British flags bordered the square. Everybody had turned up, from the children with short shorts and knocky knees to an aged woman in her rickety wheelchair.

General Beverage twitched his proud moustache.

"What you are about to do, troops, is the proudest thing a man can do."

"Erm… second proudest," piped up a little blond-haired chap from behind the general.

General Beverage twisted on his heels, enraged. "HOW DARE YOU INTERRUPT ME, BOY! Darn shame you aren't a few years older." The general took a twist of Casper's cheek and squeezed. "Yes," he sneered, "nearly ripe for the trenches."

Casper shivered. "Listen, sorry and everything, but I need your army. We've got this giant robot destroying the village, and only Corne-on-the-Kobb's best can save us."

"I see…" General Beverage gritted his teeth. "This might be just the training session we need before heading to the front. Men, quick march!"

The Great Tiramisu's homecoming performance had long been awaited and much hyped. But now the day had come, and there was the greasy Italian magician himself, kinder and gentler than before, but with the same grand aplomb that the public loved so much.

This trick involved his beloved white tiger bouncing on a trampoline while The Great Tiramisu juggled seven flaming batons. Then *PAFF*, the tiger was slung over The Great Tiramisu's shoulder, and jumping on the trampoline was... Casper Candlewacks.

"Oh," said Casper. "Hi."

The greasy Italian took less than a second to recover from his shock. "Aha!" he cried. "It'sa magic!" He took a long bow as the crowd erupted.

Casper climbed off the trampoline and approached the magician. "Can I use you for a second? And your animals? We can be back five minutes ago if you really want to impress the crowd."

The Great Tiramisu eyed Casper cheekily. Then, "Ah, I cannot-a resist. Where we go?"

And with a puff of smoke, they disappeared backstage.

13 June 1541, getting on for afternoon tea

"Lambs' knees! Getcha lambs' knees! One

shilling per sack!"

"Rotten apples! Nice an' brown. Practically giving these away now. Maggots'll be a penny extra."

The place stank. Casper had never seen, or smelt, the Corne-on-the-Kobb village square so heaving with humanity. Market traders hawked their wares to the filthy public that passed hungrily by. Urchin boys pattered around holding handfuls of rats by the tail while a wrinkly-skinned woman in a frilly bonnet poured buckets of brown muck from a high window. Goats roasted on spits, men spat on goats, and Casper trod in something slippery that gave off a musky smell like an old plimsoll full of cheese.

Forcing back the bubbling in his throat, Casper clambered up the wooden steps to the gallows and cleared his throat. "Hey!" he shouted. "Who wants a fight?"

"WE DO!" roared back a good chunk of the village.

"Great! Then follow me!"

And they did, with cleavers, ropes or buckets of slop, shouting foul Tudor obscenities and singing tavern songs.

30 May 2013, just before supper time

Julius Candlewacks stuck a finger in his vat of soup and sucked it. "What does it need?" he asked, partly to himself and partly to Cuddles, who had been taped to his kitchen wall.

"TATATA!" screamed Cuddles.

"It needs something." Julius

238

racked his brains. "A little… fishiness. That's it." He always kept a mackerel in the freezer for such occasions.

But on turning round, he found that there were three more people in his kitchen, one of them being his son. Julius didn't keep up with Casper's schoolfriends, and he certainly didn't remember the names of these two, so he smiled amiably, but directed his speech towards Casper.

"Casp! Hi, chief." Julius gave Casper a rough little head-scratch, and found his fingers stuck.

"Hey, Dad. Can we take Cuddles? We need her for… erm…"

"Hard disk space," said a chunky girl with one hell of a nose.

That sounded like a computer thing, so Julius nodded sagely. "You kids and your Wi-Fi. Go on, take her off my hands."

And like that, they'd grabbed her and gone.

9 July 3781, Consumption Protocol 2

"Now this is the *real* future."

Casper stepped off the holographic kerb just as a sleek silver hover-board hummed past. Its driver, a skinny woman in a skintight jumpsuit with a full UV face mask, turned to Casper and shrieked, "Malware scum!"

Flanella was trying to log on to the postbox, but she needed a password.

The statue in the centre of Corne-on-the-Kobb's neon village square had a television for a head, screeching out blindingly vibrant adverts for the latest must-have products: Terrabyte-Pops and HD Donuts.

"Here, look, Casper," called Chrys. "Flanella's hacked it."

The screen of the postbox now read: Do you want to summon the Peace Protection Squad?

The moment Flanella pressed Yes, possibly even a moment before, six men in full polymer body armour zapped out of thin air and saluted.

"Your request, ma'am?" said the one with a red stripe on his helmet. Casper guessed he was in charge.

"We got a giant robot being a baddie, mister," said Flanella. "In the past."

"This sounds like a job for –" the other five men joined the first to point to the sky and shout – "PEACE PROTECTION SQUAD!" Then rockets fired from their feet and they shot off into the sky.

Casper faltered. "Are they coming?"

"I guess we'll meet them at the bus stop," grimaced Chrys.

16 December 2014, gone lunchtime

"Mum, you there?"

Amanda looked up from her knitting and gasped. "Caspy! You look so young!"

Maybe it was the hair, or how flushed his face was, or the fact that he was with girls and probably showing off, but Casper had lost a good two years

242

from his face since she saw him this morning. "Er... yes," he said, his voice suddenly going growly and low. "It's the light. Anyway, where's Cuddles?"

"In her room. Eating a puzzle. Do you need her?"

She never got an answer. Casper and his friends flew upstairs, grabbed Cuddles and dragged her kicking and screaming from the house.

Within hours, well, minutes, well, centuries, depending on how you measure time and stuff, the Candlewacks kitchen was full to bursting with hundreds of willing rebels from the past, present and future of Corne-on-the-Kobb.

Mayors, mayoresses, butchers, butcheresses, bakers, three different versions of Cuddles

Candlewacks and an angry-looking goat shouted their support for Casper's cause and stamped their feet on the poor kitchen floor.

"Excuse me!" shouted Casper as loudly as his lungs would let him. "Could you all be quiet for a minute?"

"Hear hear!" shouted Audrey Snugglepuss.

"Quite agree!" agreed tiny Mitch McMassive.

"Not at all!" roared Mayor Rattsbulge. "We should be loud!"

"I cannot-a hear de boy!" The Great Tiramisu tried to hush his yelping walrus.

"Anybody seen my goat?" shouted Sandy Landscape.

And then the place descended into chaos for the third time this minute.

Casper stood down from his chair and sagged.

"You're doing brill!" said Flanella. "Malcolm detects a seventy-two per cent rise in motivation since you stopped speaking."

"It's going terribly, and you all know it." Casper surveyed the sea of faces with despair. Half of them didn't know who he was, one or two were demanding cash-in-hand payments, and a group in the corner thought this was a package holiday to Malaga. It was a nightmare.

WHEEEE-SPACKK!

The crowd screamed and ducked for cover as Betty Woons let off one of her firework-flavoured jelly beans.

"Lishten ter the boy!" the old woman croaked.

When they looked up again, Casper was back on his chair.

"Now listen," he began, his heart drumming out

a samba rhythm on the inside of his ears. "I can tell you're all excited. And that's good. But let's save it for tomorrow."

The crowd nodded. He'd finally got their attention.

"This may not feel like your village. It's probably seen better days, to be honest. But that's why you're all here. Because this *is* your village, or at least it's supposed to be. Corne-on-the-Kobb's supposed to be a place of freedom and fun, and most of all, idiocy."

At the word 'idiocy', the crowd all nodded solemnly.

"But Briar Blight's not letting it be that way. Briar's not letting us be idiots. And we won't have it!"

"We won't have it!" cheered the crowd.

"Tomorrow, we're going to take that factory down and free our friends. But it's easier said than done. You see, they've got this, how do I put it... They might have a giant-ish robot."

The crowd stirred.

"How giant-ish?" asked an old-fashioned man with a fluffy collar.

"Let's not think about that." Casper laughed awkwardly. "We have a plan to even the field. While you guys draw the, ahem, slightly-over-average-sized robot out from its lair, three of us will scale the thing and take it out of commission."

"So you won't be with us in the battle?" cried a girl in a metallic cape and snazzy sunglasses.

"He's abandoning us!" wailed a man astride a horse.

"We'll lose for sure!"

"Without him we're nothing!"

And the place descended into mayhem once more, but more sobby this time.

Casper sighed. "Ah well. I did my best."

"If we're going to climb that robot, there has to be someone on the ground," Chrys grimaced. "Look at them, they need a leader."

The answer popped into Casper's brain like freshly toasted toast. "We need to take one last trip in the Time Toaster."

Chapter Minus 637

Sir Gossamer

4 August 1374, second breakfast

"You sure this is the place?" Chrys raised a doubtful eyebrow.

"We got the right year," nodded Casper. "I remember it from the stories: 'In 1374, brave Sir Gossamer D'Glaze and his wife established their first settlement beside the River Kobb, which would grow to become the village we now know as Corne-on-the-Kobb.' It should be right here."

But even as he spoke, he was beginning to doubt it. Gone was the square and the houses and the looming Blight Manor. This far back, all Casper could see was a small mud hut with a thatched roof, set beside a rippling stream and a cow tied to a post.

"Hello?" called Casper, approaching the hut's opening. "We're looking for Sir Gossamer D'Glaze. He's eight feet tall, muscles up to his eyes and he rides a great black stallion. Do you know him?"

A woman's voice giggled from halfway up a nearby apple tree.

"Hey!" came a squeak from inside the hut. "What's so funny?"

A grubby young man emerged from the hut,

spotty and lanky like a skeleton in a skin suit. He stood at a funny angle and three gappy teeth poked out between his lips.

"Hi," said Casper. "Is your dad in? We're looking for Sir Gossamer."

"That's me." The young man scratched his head and sniffed the finger. "Goss D'Glaze at yer service. But I ain't no sir."

"Evidently," snorted Chrys.

"But this is wrong…" whispered Casper. "He's supposed to be massive and gallant, and ride a huge stallion."

"I got this cow," said Goss proudly. "She's called Pigge."

Flanella had wandered over to the apple tree.

She gave the trunk a shake and a woman fell out.

"Watch it!" snapped the woman as a dozen apples fell from their stalks and bonked herself and Flanella on the head.

Flanella looked disappointed. "Thought you were a talking tree," she said.

"Well, I ain't!" Then the girl turned to the other two visitors, and Casper got to see her face. Wiry and rough, but with a set of sparkling eyes that he seemed to recognise.

And then it hit him.

"Betty?" He choked.

"Aye," she said with a curt nod. "Oo's askin'?"

Casper gave a grin. Betty Woons! In the Middle Ages! "I mean, I knew you were *old*, but…"

"I en't old! I'm four and twenty, not a day over." Betty clicked her teeth.

"I'm Casper, anyway. And I need to borrow your husband for a battle."

Betty collapsed in fits of giggles. "Forra battle? 'Im? Knock yerself out!"

The little Sir Gossamer stood timidly by his hut. Casper looked him up and down – and sighed. He'd have to do.

"Sir Gossamer," Casper began. "Sorry about earlier. We were expecting someone bigger." He shifted on his feet. "Listen, we need somebody to lead an army into battle. It's kind of important. We wanted to ask you."

"Me?" squeaked Goss. "I'm flattered, but…"

"Yeah, thought not," said Chrys. "Bye, then." She turned to leave, but Casper grabbed her elbow.

"Wait," he said. "Can't we give him a chance? You guys thought I was a hero, but look at me. You can't say I'm any better."

The spiky-haired girl surveyed Goss up and down as if he were livestock, then nodded. "Fine. Not as if we've got another option."

Casper turned to face Goss directly. "Do you think you could… I don't know… beef up a little? Build up some muscles?"

"I could try, I suppose." Goss spent thirty seconds trying to lift a nearby pot.

"Shall we leave you to it?" asked Casper.

"Could you?"

"We'll be back in, say, two years. How does that sound?"

4 August 1376, elevenses

"We're back!"

Betty screamed and dived into the river.

Goss emerged from the hut, surprised to see the visitors again. "How did you do that?"

Casper smiled. "Oh, we took a short cu— WOW!"

Goss frowned. "Wow?"

The two girls nodded. "Wow."

Goss hadn't grown an inch, but to say he'd filled out was an understatement. He had perfectly defined biceps, triceps, quadraceps and fiveceps. His glutes were tight, his abs were fab, and he could kill a man with his thighs. Casper, who two years ago had felt like his equal, now shivered in Sir Gossamer's shadow like a chilly vole.

"Do you still want me for that battle?"

The three children nodded nervously.

"Then lead the way. Betty, Pigge, you shall come too. Ah!" Sir Gossamer's gigantic arm swept to his flowing hair and flicked it back irritatedly. "I don't have a sword."

"You don't?" This was wrong. Casper knew Sir Gossamer's famed sword all too well. Big, bejewelled and very stealable. He'd seen it a thousand times as he walked past Sir Gossamer's statue in the village square. And now it was held in the golden hands of Oleander Blight in the Corne-on-the-Kobb of 2012. Well, it was only right that Sir Gossamer should have it back.

"I know where you can find the perfect sword," said Casper.

Chapter 17

The Battle of the Kobb

When dawn broke over Blight Manor, the lookouts on the morning shift all had a bit of a heart attack. A full-blown rebel army stood at the far edge of the lawn with a sole swordsman mounted on an enormous mooing steed at the head of the pack.

"Who are they?" asked one guard.

"Where did they come from?" asked another.

"What's the capital of Australia?" asked a third, who'd got the wrong idea entirely.

Casper stepped forward and turned to face his ragtag army. Armed in baking-tray breastplates and saucepan helmets or thick pairs of trousers fortified with Sellotape, they held their weapons in the air: rolling pins, battered sausages, big bags full of dung.

This felt good. Before Casper, hundreds, if not thousands, of Corne-on-the-Kobb idiots from across time were ready to defend their village. To lead them was an eleven-year-old boy with a wild imagination and a scruffy crop of wild blond hair in which many pencils and woodland creatures had been lost.

Towards the front was Sir Gossamer, sitting astride his trusty steed, Pigge. He held his bejewelled sword aloft, rising high above the crowd. A gasp rippled through the ranks and they all fell silent.

"On my signal, we advance!" roared Casper.

"What's your signal going to be?" asked a freckled chap with a hockey stick halfway back.

"Erm… it'll be…" and then a bit of pollen got up Casper's nose. "Haa-CHOO!"

And just like that, the battle began.

Villagers from times gone by and times still to come charged like wonky barbarians towards Blight Manor. The Brewster brothers reached the perimeter fence first, chucked their brother, little Snivel, straight over and clambered up after him. Not far behind was a Victorian gent in a wig with a carving knife, then Sandy Landscape and his prized pitchfork signed by Murray 'The Mulcher'

Mazeltov, then a score of racing donkeys and Cuddles Candlewacks, all teeth and razor claws. Mayor Rattsbulge came behind with his battered Cumberland sausage, flanked by two afro-sporting disco dudes in bell-bottomed trousers. Old Betty Woons and Young Betty Woons piled in after them, one pushing the other's wheelchair, both screaming horrific obscenities at the crumbling walls of Blight Manor.

Casper had wanted a response, and that's exactly what he got. Alarms sounded, bread guns *THOOM*ed and the pigeons swooped down. But the villagers had been warned and swatted the pigeons away with whatever defences they had.

Casper, Flanella and Chrys waited patiently at the rear of the battleground.

Until it was their moment, the best they could do was cheer from the sidelines.

But as the first piece of fence crushed under the weight of the idiot hordes, that screeching crunch tore from Warehouse 3 and Casper knew the bait had worked.

Up into the sky the robot loomed, perhaps even more terrifying in the light of day, now that its pointy nose glimmered in the sunlight. It turned its head upwards and shrieked its demonic battle cry, before lunging forward and firing the first salvo of freshly baked breadcrumbs at the attackers.

Now the pigeons were really interested. Clouds of them descended, tearing and snapping for chunks of the delicious dough. Villagers rolled and stamped as they tried to fend off the birds, but for every one that flew off, more would latch on.

The robot advanced, stomping one foot over the perimeter fence. Casper led the other two round the tree line, keen not to be seen as he approached the robot's leg.

"Draw him out, men!" roared Sir Gossamer, rearing Pigge and cantering back on himself.

Just as rehearsed, the front two lines of villagers split and retreated to the flanks, opening up space where the robot stood. Like waves, the troops parted from its enormous footsteps, gradually but ever so surely drawing the robot away from Blight Manor.

"EAT BREAD, MINIONS!" roared the robot in Briar Blight's guttural voice. It lumbered forward, blasting a fistful of bread at a crowd of Tudor market traders, and finding its target. The pigeons descended, but the multitudes fought on.

There were fifty metres between Blight Manor and the robot, and twenty metres between the robot and Casper. If Sir Gossamer had noticed, he should be calling the next stage of the attack. "Come on, Goss," Casper muttered. "Close it in."

"Close in!" roared Gossamer, spurring Pigge back towards the robot. "Attack yonder golem!" The order spread like margarine, and a roar rose up from the troops. The wide circle surrounding the robot contracted as Corne-on-the-Kobb's time fighters surged towards the monster from all sides. Crowds of them clustered about the robot's legs, stunting its movement. It tried to shoot straight downward, but most of the bread deflected off its thigh.

Wooden swords and cardboard arrows plinked and plonked against the robot's chrome legs.

Brutes launched denting fists into its ankles, and The Great Tiramisu cast all the spells he knew up towards its face. The attack wasn't doing much damage, but that was as expected. However, like a swarm of ants crawling up your trousers, it did a pretty good job of distracting the thing.

"Now!" Casper called, dashing forward into the fray, followed by Flanella and Chrys. They barged through battling rebels, ducked under clubs and cricket bats, right up to the enormous metal foot. Casper clambered up to the ankle and motioned for the other two to cling on. Just as Flanella hugged the back of the robot's heel, it moved again, swinging the three wildly behind it as it aimed to break free of the mob. Flanella edged further up just in time to avoid being crushed as the robot slammed its foot back down on the grass. Casper waited for the next still moment, gritted his teeth and hauled himself up to the knee. Handholds were difficult – the robot's legs were smooth and the joins were clean. The only way to make progress was to shin upwards like monkeys on a tree trunk. But monkeys had it lucky: tree trunks generally don't walk around as you try to climb them.

Casper's sweaty hands slipped as he climbed further. The robot's thigh got thicker too, making shinning up that much harder. Below, Mayor Rattsbulge was crushing the robot's toes with his gigantic frame, giving the three a few precious moments to climb as it wrestled free.

Casper edged up further. The backside hatch was in grasping distance now. A thick metal handle gave Casper his first good handhold since he left dry land, and with a hefty tug it wrenched downwards, swinging the hatch open. A blast of eyebrow-singeingly hot air forced its way out. He grabbed the lip of the hatch with one hand, and then the other. But it was a stretch, and as he wrenched himself up, his legs slipped free. Suddenly, Casper was swinging from the bum of a robot, ten metres above cold, hard ground, wishing he'd spent longer on the monkey bars at the Corne-on-the-Kobb playground and monkey-bar emporium. Chrys and Flanella hugged the robot's leg below, waiting for their turn to climb in. Casper's arms screamed with pain, his fingers starting to cramp.

"I can't hold on!" he shouted, the wind whipping his face.

Chrys wanted to say something supportive, but just shrugged.

Casper's right hand slipped. He reached up for something solid, but found only cold metal. He could feel the fingers of his left hand sweating, twitching, slipping from their hold. And then somebody from inside the hatch had grabbed his right hand, and was tugging him in. Casper scrabbled upwards with all free limbs, pushing himself gratefully with his other arm and then his knees, until the cold air of the outside had been replaced by pulsing furnace heat.

"I'm alive. I'm not squashed on the ground. I'm in a robot. This is… good."

Casper looked up to see his rescuer. A coal-smeared face with a dongly nose grinned back.

"Hello, Casper. I did a robot."

Casper and Lamp helped Chrys up into the hatch first, then did the same with Flanella.

"Thanks, grandfather," she said idly.

"No problem," Lamp replied. "Right then, should I show you around?"

The bowels of the robot were more of a coal furnace, with steaming black pipes leading up to countless fan ovens, each containing loaves of half-baked bread.

Around the place were bundles of wires and blooping light displays. Flanella picked her favourite and set to work, pulling out Casper's hacked Tickle Tag and unfolding Malcolm on a clean surface nearby to begin installation.

An intercom buzzed from a mesh in the ceiling. "Oy, Flannigan. Shovel faster. We're running out of bread."

Chrys shivered at the sound of her brother's voice.

"Yes, sir, Briar, sir!" shouted Lamp.

"What d'you think this is, a holiday camp?"

"Yes, sir, I think so, sir."

"NO! No, it's not! Now get shovelling before I hide another of your kittens."

Lamp took his spade and shovelled a few heaps of coal into the blazing furnace. "He works me hard, Casper," sighed Lamp, "but he's a fair boss. And the pay is good. I think. How much is no pounds naughty naught per hour after tax?"

Casper held a finger to his lips. "Can Briar hear us? Where is he – back in Blight Manor?"

"He's upstairs. In the head, with Alimony. You can go up there if you like." Lamp pointed his spade at a lift, built into what would be the robot's spine.

Casper's heart raced. "He's right here? Oh, goodness. Flanella, hack faster!"

Lamp got back to shovelling. "Nice of you to pop by, but I'd better get on, really. Look at all this coal I've got to spade."

"We're here to free you, Lamp."

"Oh…" He looked disappointed. "Can I finish this first?"

"For now, yes. You'd better carry on as if we're not here. Briar mustn't know."

Flanella and Malcolm were making progress. The Tickle Tag hung limply from a circuit board, but Malcolm's screen was running scripts that'd soon have it ready to *bzzt*.

The robot shook, and screams came from below. Either the pigeons had got wilder, the bread had got thicker or somebody had seen a popstar.

"There!" cried Flanella. "All logged in. Malcolm wants to know what channel the Tickle Tag's on."

All eyes went to Chrys. She shrugged.

Casper's mouth went dry. "You mean, you don't know what channel he uses?"

"He uses a lot of channels," Chrys grumbled. "Seven three six is summoning tigers, nine one zero is for a change of pants. You can't expect me to remember them all."

"But this one's kind of crucial." Casper held his hands to his forehead, desperately trying to think of a solution. "Flanella, can't you just set it to activate on any channel?"

"Course not. Can you watch all the telly channels at once?"

"If you've got enough tellies," said Casper.

"But we don't have enough tellies. We've only got one." Flanella pointed at the Tickle Tag. "Except it's not even a telly."

Malcolm made some grumbling noises. Everyone else tried to work out why they were talking about tellies.

Flanella spoke up again. "Malcolm says he needs the channel, and he can't work without it.'

"But we don't know it! And we don't have time to guess them all." Casper looked at his watch. The villagers should've overpowered the guards by now. They'd soon be on their way out, leading those freed workers. "If we can't get this working, they'll be tickled and recaptured *again*, and the robot'll be just fine."

Chrys gave a snarl. "But I've told you! I don't know the code!"

"Then there's only one thing we can do. We take that lift all the way to the head, and we try to reason with Briar."

Flanella gasped. "But I'm scared of heights."

Chrys scrunched her mouth. "I could give it a go."

"What else have we left?" This was lunacy, Casper knew, but he'd run out of time and plans.

"I'll just stay here spading," said Lamp.

The doors to the lift opened and the three squeezed inside. It was carpeted, quite posh, the sort of lift Lamp might have stolen from a hotel.

"Going up," a lady said, and the lift jerked into motion.

Ping!

The doors slid open to a chrome and ivory control room, bedecked with the latest gadgets and lots of flashing lights, which probably did nothing, but looked absolutely brilliant. Briar and Anemonie Blight swivelled round in their black pilots' chairs to face their intruders.

"Lamp, what on earth do you want n— AAARGH!" Anemonie screamed.

Briar reached for his bread gun.

"Stop!" cried Chrys.

"Why should I?" Briar's lips bent into a sickly smile. "Traitor."

"Am I, though?" Chrys snarled. "Or have I just brought you the two most wanted rebels in Corne-on-the-Kobb, unarmed, without even lifting a finger?"

Time seemed to stop. Casper turned to Chrys, saw her cruel eyes, and his heart sank. "What? How could you…"

"Oh, deary me, Candlewacks," sniggered Anemonie. "Did you make the mistake of trusting a Blight? Tut tut." She wrinkled her pointy nose.

Chrys walked slowly to the other side to join her brother and grandmother.

"What's she doing?" asked Flanella. "Chrys, you're on the wrong side, silly."

The lift doors slid closed softly behind them, and Casper knew he and Flanella were trapped.

"Your little rebellion was so much fun to crush," smiled Briar. "Shame it had to end so soon, really. Oh, look, another escape attempt." He dragged right on a joystick and the robot swung hard with his movement. From up here, through the glass windscreen, Casper could see it all: Blight Manor, the battle, the pigeons... By now the fence-cutting team had done their job, and through gaps in the wire poured streams of freed workers.

"Ah, and you did so well. Look, some of my employees have escaped once more," Briar chuckled. "You can't even tell which is which." He pulled the remote control from his jacket pocket. "Well, there's always one way to separate them." Briar tapped in a three-digit code and exactly half the ant-like figures collapsed into fits of giggles.

Beside him, Chrys watched her brother tickle his minions with victory in her eyes.

"You're *evil*," muttered Casper.

"I know!" Briar's voice had a note of celebration. "And it never gets old!" He pushed the VOLUME UP button and the giggling got louder.

"I've got what I've always wanted here, Candlewacks," smirked Anemonie. "Respect, success, and bags and bags of money. I ain't letting you take that away from me."

Chrys sniggered. "I feel sorry for you, Casper." She looked him straight in the eye. "Too stupid to go free when I gave you the chance."

"When was my chance?" asked Casper, confused. "In the kitchen? To escape in the Time Toaster?"

"You could be far away now. A Saxon shepherd, perhaps. But, no, you decide to stay and lose even more."

Casper shook his head. "You're the worst of them all, Chrys."

"As I say," Chrys spoke more slowly now, more deliberately. "I feel sorry *for* you. *Too* stupid to go *free*."

"I heard you the first time."

"But did you?" She winked at Casper. "Did you

really hear me? I feel so sorry *for* you. *Too* stupid to go *free.*"

"Stop saying that! Why are you… What's with the…" and then he saw where Chrys was leaning on the dashboard, and he swallowed his questions.

There was a big red button marked INTERCOM, and Chrys's palm had pressed firmly down on it. Whatever they were saying, Lamp could hear. Then there were the words she was using, more specifically, the ones she was stressing. "*For… too… free. For… too… free.*"

Casper had to bite his tongue to force back the smile. *Four, two, three!* They were numbers! They were… *a channel*. Casper got it now. Chrys had gone over to Briar's side, but only to find out the channel for the Tickle Tags. And there it was, hidden in her words. *Four, two, three!* And, as

Casper looked, Briar pressed those exact numbers as he tickled the workers on the ground once again.

Now all that was needed was for Lamp to decipher Chrys's secret message. He could hear her on the intercom, yes, but Lamp's code-breaking skills were limited by his word-understanding skills, which were limited by his brain-thinking skills. Oh dear.

In the meantime, bread rained down on the villagers. The pigeons made a grey blanket over the lawn now.

"You know what, Briar? If Flanella had a computer right now, she'd take this whole place down," Casper said, nice and loud so that Lamp would hear.

"Maybe she would," agreed Chrys, speaking more closely to the intercom now, "but we'd never give her that chance. *For* you'd need *to* get *free* from the Blights before you'd get close to another computer."

"My 'puter's downstairs," said Flanella. "I could go and get it."

Briar raised his bread gun. "You're going nowhere."

Still nothing. Casper watched the intercom and willed Lamp to hear his thoughts. *Just type four two three! Just do it!*

Flanella had lost interest and was counting her fingers.

Below, breaded villagers and workers alike were being dragged back into Blight Manor by the burly guards. The pigeons had lifted The Great Tiramisu's white tiger into a tree. Three of the Cuddleses had amassed a pile of pigeons to rival Mount Everest, but their claws were growing blunt and still flocks of the vermin bombarded them. Guards and Brewsters threw punches and breadcrumbs until both were floored by the sweeping foot of the robot. There was no more time to play around.

"For goodness' sake, Lamp, the code's four two three! Type it into the computer! Do it n—"

Briar was on Casper before he could finish the sentence, bundling him to the ground and covering his mouth. Anemonie finally caught wind and snatched Chrys's hand away from the intercom, shouting "TRAITOR! DOUBLE TRAITOR!"

Flanella lost count at eleven and started again.

Casper wasn't sure if it was Briar, the robot, or the ground beneath the robot's feet, but at that moment things began to shake. They all slid towards the control panel, then tumbled back towards the lift. Anemonie lost her footing, tumbling into Chrys. Briar threw a punch at Casper, but the cabin upturned, Briar rolled backwards and his wayward fist struck Anemonie's jaw. A huge rumbly burp bubbled from below and the cabin shook once more.

"Lamp's done it!" cried Casper. "The robot's being tickled!"

Flanella giggled. "I forgot which way was up!"

Then the floor tipped so far upwards it was now a wall, and Casper found himself and the others tumbling into the lift. The doors closed, the nice lady said "Going down," and then the robot swung the other way. The lift's five passengers crunched together on one mirrored wall. The robot tilted again. Casper thought he'd got a mouthful of

Anemonie's hair. Briar threw another punch, this time clocking himself plum on the nose.

Ping!

The door slid open and the five, shuffled like a pack of cards, flew downwards, or upwards, or whichever wards it was at this point (quite frankly I've lost track of it all), out into Lamp's bakery room.

Lamp, upside down, looked pleased to have visitors, but his glee only lasted until the robot plummeted downwards and everybody's stomachs floated up to their throats.

Then – *KABOOSH!*

The impact threw all six up into the air and crashing back in a dizzy heap.

Outside, Casper could hear the strained cheers of hundreds of villagers. Inside, the lights had failed and somebody was strangling him.

"Get off!" choked Casper.

"Oh, sorry," came the grunt of Chrys. "Thought you were my brother."

"No, you oaf of a girl. I'm over here."

Chrys clambered over the pile of bodies and strangled Briar instead.

Then the backside hatch flew open, flooding

the bakery room with sunlight, and the chiselled face of Sir Gossamer peeped in. "Hark! They're in here!"

A heartfelt roar burst from the crowd, and then more and more heads popped over the edge.

"It's Casper!" cried Sandy Landscape.

"And the others too!" squeaked Mitch McMassive.

"Bring me the Blights!" roared the crumb-faced Mayor Rattsbulge.

Baz and Gaz Lazlo lifted each person out of the furnace room in turn, throwing them either on a pile marked HEROES or one marked VILLAINS. At first, Chrys was thrown on the VILLAINS pile, but that was soon sorted out.

Blinking in the sunlight, Casper sat himself up on the robot's metal back and looked at the scene surrounding him. Both of the robot's arms had fallen off in the impact and spilt dozens of freshly baked loaves all over the grass. The pigeons had given up on their first course, left the villagers alone and flocked to the far thicker pickings there.

Now free of pigeons, the crowds of crumb-encrusted villagers were jumping up and down, hugging each other and clonking their swords merrily on the robot's dead shell.

Briar and Anemonie were thrust under Baz and Gaz's sweaty armpits and carried down from the robot, screaming vile curses as they went. Around them, the recently resigned employees of Blight Enterprises ripped off their Tickle Tags and stamped on them until all that was left was microchips.

"Lock 'em in the stocks!" shouted Sir Gossamer.

"Chuck 'em in the deepest cell the Kobb Valley's got to offer!" roared Mayor Rattsbulge.

"Chop orf their heads!" screeched Clemmie Answorth, swinging her handbag above her head like a perfumed mace.

An exhausted smile spread over Casper's lips as he saw the victorious scene on the lawn. He'd done it. The village was safe once more. Even the

guards of Blight Manor had dropped their bread guns and fled once the robot had fallen.

The four burly Brewster brothers lumbered forward and picked up Casper, Chrys, Flanella and Lamp in turn. Lifting them high above their heads, they began a parade around the lawn, a mass of hundreds of freed slaves and time-shifted villagers cheering their names.

"It's Casper Candlewacks!" cried a girl in grey overalls.

"And Lamp Flannigan!" cried another. "They're so dreamy!"

Below them, villagers reached out to touch their heroes, screaming as if they'd met a popstar.

"I could get used to this," smiled Casper.

Chrys flashed Casper a rare smirk. "Sorry about double-crossing you. I had to get the code somehow."

Casper shook his head. "It was clever! You've got some serious brains up there."

Chrys scratched her spiky-haired head. "Thanks."

"Think you could steer your brother's company into something more worthwhile than spit-water?"

"I've picked up enough from Briar to give it

a go. But I'd need an assistant. Flanella, want a job?"

Flanella replied with a geeky snort. "Do I get a name badge?"

"We can discuss that tomorrow."

"Because I love name badges. Malcolm wants one too."

Casper hopped down from the hands of the villagers carrying him when he saw the four Cuddleses and Julius with his sharpened spatula.

"I did it, Dad! I saved the village."

Julius ruffled Casper's messy blond hair. "Again. You're making quite a habit of it."

The crowds encircled Casper, reaching in to ruffle his hair as well.

"You saved us!" an old lady cheered.

"You healed my foot!" claimed a man who'd

just thrown away his pair of crutches.

"You found my goat!" shouted Sandy Landscape, a braying goat slung over his shoulders.

Lamp lolloped over to Casper, coal-smeared, but happy. "Hey, Casper. I worked it out. We're in the future, aren't we?"

"Yes, you genius, but not for long. We've got to return all these people to their normal times before this whole thing gets very complicated. Ready to help me pilot that Time Toaster of yours?"

"Cor, d'you fix it?" Lamp looked impressed.

"Not quite," admitted Casper. "Betty Woons had a spare. No idea where she got that one from, though."

Lamp shrugged. "Time Toaster shop?"

"Maybe," Casper clapped his hands together. "Anyway, who's first?"

A couple dressed in black and white from the twenties shuffled forward silently.

"All right, you're as good as any." He called to the rest of the crowd. "If you'd all come this way, we've got a bus to catch."

"There's nothing else for it," said Lamp. "*Let's TIME!*"

THE END

Epilogue

"Well, I think you're the last of them."

Casper and Lamp led Betty and Pigge out of the smoking bus stop, with Goss strutting behind.

"This ain't my Corne-onna-Kobb," cackled Betty. "Too many 'ouses. Not 'nuff peace 'n' quiet."

"You don't understand," said Casper. "This isn't where you get off. It's *our* stop."

Goss frowned. "I don't understand. How do we get home?"

"Easy, just pull that lever. I've already set it to

the right coordinates."

Betty hopped from foot to foot with unease.
"Fanks, but… issa bit ugly to have hangin' around.
D'you wanna hang on ter it?"

"We can't," said Casper. "I've seen me and
Lamp in the future, and we've got some serious

wrinkles. We take the long way round. No more short cuts for us. But you… Betty, you've been there at every single point in Corne-on-the-Kobb history I've visited with this Time Toaster! I didn't know why at first, but now I think I've got it."

"'Av yer?" Betty did a clueless face.

"Looks to me like you're going to have an awful lot of use for that machine in your life. Perhaps you could pop back and forth to all the Corne-on-the-Kobbs through time. Make sure everything's in order. You can give it back to me when you're a little older."

Betty nodded. "I'll keep it safe, lad. Dontcher worry."

"And Sir Gossamer?"

Goss stepped forward. "Yes, my lord?"

"Keep the village safe. It's special to me."

"Which village is that?"

"The one you're about to build. For all your children."

"Ah," said Goss. "That one."

THE END

Another Epilogue

Three days later, a little stall appeared on the Corne-on-the-Kobb village square, run by the charming Anemonie Blight. She was selling bottles of purified Kobb river water, with a secret ingredient that promised to deliver a drop of nobility in every bottle. *Essence of Nobility*, she called it, and it sold like hot cakes. It sold better than hot cakes, in fact, until Audrey Snugglepuss's hot cakes stall across the square went out of business.

"Have you seen what Anemonie's up to?" sighed Casper, plonking himself down on a greasy cushion in Lamp's garage.

"I know!" chortled Lamp. "Wish I'd thought of it first. Anyway, I've been thinking about all those gadgets we saw in the future."

"What, you mean like the bread guns?"

"Yeah, and the Tickle Tags."

Casper shivered. "Me too. Glad to be free of them, I'll say."

"Oh, me too. Anyway, I wondered how they worked, so I thought I'd knock up a couple myself. Look!" With his left hand, Lamp held up a black hairdryer with a battery pack and a pouch filled with breadcrumbs. In his right, a small ankle bracelet

from his mum's jewellery drawer bleeped its red winking eye. "Want to try them out?"

THE END

NO, REALLY, I'M SERIOUS.

THE END

CHAPTER 1

The Big Dog
Who Wouldn't Stop
Eating Muffins

Read more
CASPER CANDLEWACKS
Adventures

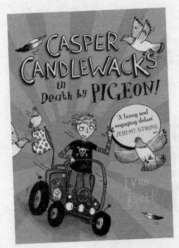